Stan said.

"I try not to kiss anyone I don't like," Jenna replied with a shrug.

Stan grinned. She was so snooty. He felt like teaching Jenna Jean a thing or two. "I have a rule for kissing." He lowered his mouth closer to hers. "Never kiss for more than thirty seconds."

His brown eyes held a wicked glint of challenge. "C'mon, Jenna Jean, it's only thirty seconds," he muttered, his mouth almost brushing hers.

The arousal in his eyes made her chest feel tight. "I—"

His mouth took hers, and Jenna widened her eyes. *What was she doing kissing Stan Michaels?*

Sensation won over thought, and she sank into the kiss.

He pulled back and swore under his breath.

"You're making me change my rule, Jenna Jean. Thirty seconds isn't nearly long enough with you."

Dear Reader,

THE BLACK WATCH returns! The men you found so intriguing are now joined by women who are also part of this secret organization created by BJ James. Look for them in *Whispers in the Dark*, this month's MAN OF THE MONTH.

Leanne Banks's delightful miniseries HOW TO CATCH A PRINCESS—all about three childhood friends who kiss a lot of frogs before they each meet their handsome prince— continues with *The You-Can't-Make-Me Bride*. And Elizabeth Bevarly's series THE FAMILY McCORMICK concludes with *Georgia Meets Her Groom*. Romance blooms as the McCormick family is finally reunited.

Peggy Moreland's tantalizing miniseries TROUBLE IN TEXAS begins this month with *Marry Me, Cowboy*. When the men of Temptation, Texas, decide they want wives, they find them the newfangled way—they *advertise!*

A Western from Jackie Merritt is always a treat, so I'm excited about this month's *Wind River Ranch*—it's ultrasensuous and totally compelling. And the month is completed with *Wedding Planner Tames Rancher!*, an engaging romp by Pamela Ingrahm. There's nothing better than curling up with a Silhouette Desire book, so enjoy!

Regards,

Lucia Macro

Senior Editor

Please address questions and book requests to:
Silhouette Reader Service
U.S.: 3010 Walden Ave., P.O. Box 1325, Buffalo, NY 14269
Canadian: P.O. Box 609, Fort Erie, Ont. L2A 5X3

LEANNE BANKS
THE YOU-CAN'T-MAKE-ME BRIDE

SILHOUETTE *Desire*

Published by Silhouette Books

America's Publisher of Contemporary Romance

SILHOUETTE BOOKS

ISBN 0-373-76082-5

THE YOU-CAN'T-MAKE-ME BRIDE

Books by Leanne Banks

Silhouette Desire

*Ridge: The Avenger #987
†The Five-Minute Bride #1058
†The Troublemaker Bride #1070
†The You-Can't-Make-Me Bride #1082

Silhouette Special Edition

A Date With Dr. Frankenstein #983
Expectant Father #1028

*Sons and Lovers
†How To Catch a Princess

LEANNE BANKS

is a national number-one bestselling author of romance. Recognized for her sensual writing with a Career Achievement Award from *Romantic Times* magazine, Leanne likes creating a story with a few grins, a generous kick of sensuality and characters that hang around after the book is finished. The "How To Catch a Princess" trilogy was inspired by Leanne's memories of her childhood and is set in Roanoke, Virginia, where Leanne grew up. Leanne loves to hear from readers. You can write to her at P.O. Box 1442, Midlothian, VA 23113.

Acknowledgments to Chief Assistant Commonwealth Attorney Betty Jo Anthony, Dee at West End Orthopedic Clinic, Chesterfield County Court Services, and Betty Minyard, for instant information on Roanoke (Thanks, Mom!).

This book is dedicated to my favorite determined teenage hero, my son, Adam Banks. It takes a special person to make us step out of our comfort zones. Your imagination, dreams and persistence inspire. Oh, how you make me grow.

Prologue

"What does it feel like to be twelve years old?"

In the glow of the flashlight, Jenna Jean Anderson thought about it, then looked at her friends Emily and Maddie and shrugged. "I don't know. Older than eleven, I guess."

"Almost a teenager," Maddie cooed.

"My mother says I get to wear lipstick when I turn twelve," ten-year-old Emily, who wore a frilly night-gown, told them.

"I probably won't be able to wear lipstick until I turn eighteen," Maddie said in a mournful tone. Poor Maddie was always getting grounded.

Jenna Jean was mildly curious about lipstick, but so far, turning twelve meant she'd be baby-sitting her five younger brothers this summer.

At least her mother had allowed her to have a

sleepover in the backyard. It was the only way to keep her brothers out of her hair. Earlier this afternoon, she'd thrown the old bedspread over the clothesline, put a blanket on the ground and stocked the tent with two flashlights, her transistor radio, Kool-Aid and cookies. Her brothers had tried to snitch the cookies.

She glanced at her watch. "I want to stay up until two o'clock in the morning," she told her friends.

"My mother says you get bags under your eyes if you don't get enough sleep," Emily said.

"Old people get bags," Maddie said.

"Well, Jenna Jean's old now. So she might get bags."

Maddie shone the flashlight in Jenna's eyes. "I don't see any yet."

Jenna Jean ducked away from the light. "I don't care if I get bags. I want to stay awake. What do you want to do? Play truth or dare?"

Maddie pulled out a paper bag. "I brought Old Maid cards and my official fan member kit from Davey Rogers and the Pink Bubblegum rock band."

Emily smiled. "I brought my tiara." She carefully put it on Jenna Jean's head. "You should wear it since it's your birthday."

Jenna Jean felt a little silly wearing the tiara, but she still liked it, so she kept it on. "Thanks. I'll turn on the—"

"Jenna Jean," a voice outside the tent called.

Jenna Jean groaned. It was the voice of her nightmares.

Maddie's eyes rounded. "It's Stanley Michaels," she whispered.

"Jenna Jean, Jenna Jean. Sunken chest, a pirate's dream."

Totally embarrassed, Jenna Jean stood. She knew she was tall and skinny and had stringy brown hair, but it hadn't been a problem until recently. "I'm gonna kill him. I'm gonna smash his ugly face."

Emily cringed. "Maybe he has a crush on you."

That was her worst nightmare. Stanley was the meanest boy on Cherry Lane. "Ever since he grew four inches and beat me in one-on-one, he's turned into a stupid bully. He was nicer when he was shorter and his mother made him take tap dance lessons."

"I wish I could take tap," Maddie said forlornly.

"What's wrong, Jenna Jean? You scared?" Stanley taunted as he stuck his face under a corner of the bedspread, then sprinted away.

Outraged, Jenna Jean raced out of the tent after him. She wished she was still taller than Stanley. She was going to teach him a lesson. She was going to— Something hit her, and she was flat on her back with Stanley holding her down and grinning at her like a goon.

She struggled against him to no avail. "Let me go, you stupid nerd!"

"Give me your cookies, or I'll spit in your face."

She shook her head adamantly and glared at him. "You are the worst excuse for a boy in the world. You're going to be a juvenile delinquent and spend your whole life in jail."

"Give me the cookies," he demanded, holding her down.

She struggled uselessly against him. Tears sprang

to her eyes. She would do anything not to cry. Bucking against him, she chose the only solution and hated herself even as she did it. It was something one of her little brothers would have done. Whipping her head to the side, she sank her teeth into Stanley's hand and bit hard.

Stanley howled in shock, but Jenna Jean didn't let go until he begged. Swearing and nearly crying, he clutched his hand and ran home.

Jenna Jean took a deep breath as Maddie and Emily scurried to her side and pulled her to her feet.

"You were brave. I was gonna hit him with the flashlight," Maddie said.

Emily nodded. "You must have bit him hard. You've got blood on your chin."

Jenna Jean wiped her chin and looked at her fingers. Her stomach turned. "Oh no! I've got Stanley Michaels's blood in my mouth! Gross!" She spit into the grass. "I'm gonna be sick." She spit some more just to be sure she got rid of all the germs.

"Drink some Kool-Aid." Emily offered Jenna Jean a fresh paper cup. She looked around with the flashlight and found the tiara. "I hope Stanley Michaels has to get stitches. Then he'll have to get a shot."

"Maybe he'll get rabies," Maddie suggested.

Jenna Jean rolled her eyes. "I don't have rabies. Animals give you rabies."

"Oh." Maddie shrugged while Emily put the tiara back on Jenna Jean's head.

"Now, you're the birthday princess again," Emily told her.

"I don't want to be princess," Jenna Jean said, thinking about that mean Stanley Michaels. "I want to be queen."

One

Almost queen.

Almost a judge.

The commonwealth attorney had given Jenna the nod. She'd been assistant commonwealth attorney for only two years, but she had an impressive record. With no social life, aside from a few visits with her long-term friends Emily and Maddie, she'd sacrificed for every success.

Jenna knew she was young, but she was so close to getting what she'd worked for she could taste it.

Unfortunately, so could her co-workers. She stifled a sigh as she dribbled down the YMCA basketball court. Since she'd been appointed assistant C.A., Jenna had learned to take the expression "playing with the big boys" literally. The guys gave her less grief if she occasionally went a few rounds of racquetball or played basketball with them. Considering it part of the job, she was thankful for her years on the high school girls' basketball team.

"Keep your hands to yourself, Winnie," she warned Edward Winthrop, a malpractice attorney with a nasty habit of pinching.

Winnie leered. "You bring out the best in me."

Dodging him, she tossed the ball to her teammate, a new law clerk, and headed closer to the basket.

The clerk got cornered and passed the ball back to her. Jenna saw a hole in the other team's defense and went for it. She jumped forward and high, reaching and shooting. As the ball left her hands, Winnie bounced into her, and Jenna came down hard. A shocking stab of pain took her breath, and she heard a crunching sound in her ankle.

"Two points. You're eating her dust," the clerk said in a goading voice. He gave a whoop of glee.

Somebody swore at him and snatched the ball.

Jenna thought about trying to move and she nearly cried. "Omigod." Closing her eyes, she felt the men crowd around her.

"Hey, Jen, what's the—"

She heard him pause and swear. It must be horrible, she thought, and felt her stomach roll.

"For Pete's sake, she's bleeding."

Oh, no. She bit her lip. She hated the sight of blood, particularly her own.

"Is that a bone sticking through her skin?"

At that point Jenna took the easy way out and did something she'd never done before. She fainted.

When she came to, she was in ER, then radiology,

then ER again. She faded in and out during the whole miserable process.

"It's nice to see you tonight, Doctor," the nurse said. "This patient's in luck with you on call. She has a compound fracture."

"Thanks, Riley. Check OR availability and we'll go ahead and set it," a male voice replied. "She's gonna hurt like hell when she wakes up."

"She already does," Jenna announced in a voice rusty to her own ears. Her eyes remained stubbornly closed.

She heard the rustling of papers, then a muffled chuckle.

"Ms. Anderson, I'm Dr. Michaels, and I'll be taking care of you. If we've got good timing, then we'll get you into surgery tonight. I'll reposition the bone, sew you up and stabilize your ankle with a cast."

Relief rushed through her. It was one of her secret quirks, but Jenna made an initial judgment about a man based on his voice, and she liked his. It wasn't oily or harsh like the voices of some of her colleagues. Smooth as honey, his voice was deep and reassuring. It said "trust me, sweetheart." He probably had women begging to bear his children, she thought wryly. Even in her drugged state, she thought she'd detected a note of gushiness in the nurse's voice. Struggling to open her heavy lids, Jenna felt him do a quick check of her reflexes, warm gentle hands on her cool skin.

"Riley told me you were injured playing basketball. A little one-on-one?"

"No," she managed. "Full court." She squinted her eyes at him, but he looked blurry. Remembering someone giving her something for pain, she tried to focus. He seemed vaguely familiar.

"Still showing off?" He touched the area around her injury, and she reached for the ceiling.

"Whoa." He gently but firmly pressed her shoulder back down to the bed.

Amazing how undiluted pain clears one's vision. Jenna looked at his hand. It was large and strong looking with a serrated white scar across the knuckles. She frowned at that.

She shot a glance at his face and stared at him. As he bent over her, his straight, too-long-for-the-boardroom dark hair dipped over his forehead. His eyes were deep brown, concentrated and shadowed by black spiky eyelashes. She would bet he didn't miss much. His face was a masculine mix of rough-hewn bones, an expressive mouth with a full lower lip and a strong chin with a cleft. The cleft tugged at her memory, and she suddenly realized she was staring into a grown-up, more attractive version of— She looked at his hand again in alarm. "Stanley Michaels!" she shrieked.

"Don't even think about biting my hand again. And it's Dr. Stan Michaels." His voice was firm, yet laced with humor.

Astonished, she shook her head. "You're not a doctor?" She couldn't believe it. It didn't seem possible.

"I am. You can check my academic record at the University of Virginia Medical School," he assured her. "You sound surprised, Jenna Jean."

"Jenna," she corrected, then added, "And yes, I'm surprised."

He pulled out her chart again. "Any allergies?"

"Lima beans." The shock and surprise passed, and a wave of pain rolled through her. "Can we get on with this? I feel like I'm going to throw up."

"The nurse will be here in less than a minute." He squeezed her shoulder in compassion. "So what did you expect of me?" he prompted.

"I expected you to end up in prison," she told him, not mincing words, though she suspected he was trying to distract her from her pain.

"That was during my high school career." Dr. Stan Michaels gave her a bad boy grin and nodded toward the nurse when she entered.

"We have a vacancy," she told him.

"Good. Thanks, Riley." he said.

"Some of us are going out for drinks after our shift. If you're through with your surgery, we'd love to have you," Riley continued.

Jenna was getting ready to be cut open by the boy who used to sneak into the girls' locker room, and now she was being forced to hear a woman hit on him. It was too much.

"Stanley Michaels is going to perform surgery on me!" Jenna yelled, her mouth going dry with fear.

He shrugged. "If you want to wait until tomorrow, you can get another doctor."

"Tomorrow?" she echoed, and bit back a whimper. She wasn't sure she would last fifteen more minutes. She swallowed hard. "Are you sure you know what you're doing?"

"Yes."

She squeezed her eyes shut and prayed. "Okay. Do it."

Stan patted her hand. "You'll be okay. In a little while you won't feel a thing."

People didn't feel when they were dead, she thought, and her stomach clenched.

"He's a terrific doctor," Riley said, her voice dripping admiration.

For some reason the nurse's words didn't comfort Jenna. She was fairly certain Riley's view of Stanley was skewed.

"You can start the IV drip immediately. Sorry. Count me out on the drinks," he told the nurse, then turned to Jenna with an almost affectionate glint in his eyes. "Nighty-night, Jenna Jean."

"Here's a prescription for pain medication," Stan said the following afternoon as he scrawled something on a pad and tore off the top sheet.

Jenna blinked. She still couldn't believe *Stanley Michaels* had operated on her. It was hard to get past the fact that he had been in the middle of nearly every practical joke, legal or illegal, in high school, and how he had dated two-thirds of the girls in her entire graduating class. She glanced down at her new cast and frowned. "You're sure you got everything straight down there. I won't be crooked or anything, will I?"

"Crooked?" He gave her a bland look. "You're an attorney. You won't be any more crooked than you were before."

She looked down her nose at him, which was difficult since she was flat on her back. "You always had trouble with authority figures."

"I'm a changed man," he told her. "How about you? Still biting guys who are after your cookies?"

Jenna willed herself not to blush. "I'm not often forced to use self-defense tactics. Men who want my cookies show a little more finesse these days."

"Ooh," he said. "Touché." Then his demeanor changed faster than the speed of light, and he was all doctor. "This time I'm the authority figure, Jenna Jean. You do what I say.

"I put a slit in the cast to allow for swelling, but keep your leg elevated. No weight on that ankle for eight to twelve weeks. That means crutches. When you start moving again, you'll find stairs the most difficult, so you might just want to sit and move backward, lifting your weight with your hands. Is your car manual or automatic transmission?"

Despite the fact that she was still feeling no pain, Jenna's stomach sank. She hadn't had time to consider what kind of limitations a broken ankle would place on her. "Five-speed."

He made a tsking sound that was *almost* sympathetic. "No driving. You have a husband?" He checked her chart again.

"No," she said at the same time he did.

"Friend? Roommate? Lover?"

Jenna lay perfectly still. Years ago she'd perfected the art of squirming and screaming on the inside while she froze on the outside during the childhood game of Solemn Statues. "I'll handle it," she said, although the only immediate idea that came to mind was Yellow Cab.

"In case of emergency...Maddie Palmer Blackwell." Stan stopped and glanced up at her, shaking his head. "After all these years, you're still friends with Maddie. That kid couldn't stay out of trouble."

Jenna bristled. "She's been a good friend. Why shouldn't I be?"

He shook his head again, this time more thoughtfully. "No reason. Long friendships are rare. You're lucky."

Jenna blinked. She wouldn't have expected that kind of sensitive comment from Stan, even a grown-up Stan.

"You look a little confused, Jenna Jean. Do you want me to go over the instructions again?"

"Jenna," she automatically corrected, and shook her head. "I heard you the first time. I need to keep the leg elevated."

"Most of my patients stay off work the entire three months."

"Most of your patients aren't me."

He gave her a once-over and nodded. "I won't argue with that. Still stubborn?"

"Determined," she said.

He ran his hand over the dry cast. Even though she knew the move was purely professional, it felt strange for him to touch her. It put her off balance.

"Bet you're hell on wheels in the courtroom."

"I—have been fairly successful."

He grinned. "Oh, yeah. What do they call you behind your back? Does it have something to do with *teeth?*" he asked in a honey voice that she was certain could melt women. Other women.

"No," she said without squirming. "I'm called the Knife."

He raised his eyebrows in speculation. "Sharp and quick. I bet you go for the jugular."

"Only after I've exposed it."

"Well, the Knife is gonna have to stay in the woodblock for a while. You need to stay off your feet for the next few weeks."

"If it's just pain," Jenna began.

"Pain and healing," he corrected and stood. "You've damaged it. Now give it time to heal."

Jenna sighed. "I can't stay off work. I've got a schedule that doesn't stop for lunch, let alone a broken leg."

"It's gonna have to now."

"I—"

He pressed his finger over her mouth, stopping her words and making her heart race. "Jenna Jean, trust me on this. I've got a couple of nicknames, too. One of them is Saint Stan."

"Saint?" The idea was so ludicrous she couldn't contain a husky chuckle. "Where did that come from?"

"My supernatural healing powers," he told her with a deadpan expression. "My integrity. My angelic—"

"Oh, wait a minute," Jenna said, lifting her hand for him to stop. "You don't have an angelic bone in your body."

"Some of my patients have referred to me in spiritual terms."

"As they were waking up from the anesthetic," she guessed. "Or urging you into the hereafter. What's your other nickname?"

Stan's lips tilted upward in a thigh-melting smile. "Dr. S&M, but it's just because of my initials."

Grabbing a beer, Stan looked out his apartment window at the teenage kid shooting hoops. The same kid was out every night until the wee hours. He wondered where the parents were and frowned.

He sighed and drummed his fingers on the windowpane. It had been an interesting two days, he thought wryly and shook his head. Who would have thought he would ever be treating Jenna Jean Anderson? *The Knife.* She'd always been sharp, and he suspected she could cut a defendant to ribbons if she chose.

She'd always been an intriguing mix of femininity. Too strong and too smart for most of the boys in their high school class, she'd wasted little time on her love life and focused on her academics and close friends instead. Definitely a Type A woman, one who followed the rules.

Stan understood the Type A mentality, since he had his share of it. It was the rule-following part where he differed. He preferred to make his own rules.

Jenna Jean had accomplished something he hadn't, however. She'd hung on to her friends and made a place for herself.

He envied her that because he felt rootless. After serving his internship in a West Coast medical center and his residency in Florida, he'd returned to Roanoke to find some kind of stability in his life. He hadn't been home in ages, and, though it surprised the hell out of him, he'd missed it.

When he'd left, he'd thought he would never return. Roanoke was too slow, he'd always thought. At first he'd enjoyed the faster pace of bigger cities, the variety of people and places. Eventually, however, L.A. had become too busy, and so had Miami. When his best friend died nine months ago, the shock forced Stan to reflect on the past ten years of his life.

Besides his profession, what did he have to show for the time except some good times? He realized his friends were more like acquaintances, and the women... He shook his head. He might as well have had a revolving door with a timer.

He wanted more. All the stuff he'd come to believe was hokey and unnecessary. Everything he'd yawned over. A home, good friends, a purpose, and maybe someone who counted on him. He wasn't exactly sure how to get it, but he knew it would require change.

Two

One week later Jenna watched in horror as Stan sawed off her cast. Her leg was swollen and discolored from the trauma. She struggled with an urge to cover her leg. "Why are you changing it so soon?"

"To remove your stitches and check your wound," he told her, pushing the pieces of the white cast aside. He examined the sutures. "Looks good. You've been taking your antibiotic, right?"

She nodded, frowning. "It doesn't look like my leg," she murmured. "It looks like an alien leg."

Stan chuckled. "It's just a little swollen. That's to be expected. Mary will wash it. I'll remove the stitches, then we'll put on a new cast."

Mary, the office nurse, smiled as she gently washed Jenna's leg. The soothing touch helped Jenna relax. She'd been tense since Stan walked into the room. He was clearly competent and thorough, but she was too aware of him in other ways, from the boy she'd known as a child, to the man he was now. She tried to focus on the *doctor* in Dr. Michaels. "Will I keep the new cast on until the end?"

He shook his head and began snipping the stitches. "Oh, no. We'll change it about every three weeks. X-ray every time to make sure you're healing."

Jenna closed her eyes and wished her leg had never been broken. Being incapacitated was torture. This was a hell of a way to gain the virtue of humility. "Are you sure that nickname for Dr. S&M wasn't earned by your patients?"

She opened her eyes and grimaced at her unshaven leg. "Is there *any* chance you'd let me use a razor?" she whispered to Mary.

"I would," Mary said, "but—"

A buzzer sounded, and Stan flicked on the intercom button. "I could use Mary to do the X-rays for this three-year-old," a male voice said.

"She's pretty busy here at the moment, Abernathy."

A child howled in the background. "Your two-o'clock canceled," Mary pointed out.

"Okay," Stan said. "Go ahead, but come back as soon as you can to help with the cast."

"We're short-handed today, because one of our nurses is struggling with morning sickness," he told Jenna after Mary left.

Distracted, Jenna nodded. It cost her, but she had to ask. "Is there any way I can get my hands on a razor?"

Stan's lips twitched. "You're not bothered by a little hair, are you?"

It didn't look like a little bit to her. She worked to keep her composure. "I would really like a razor."

"We don't usually shave legs in the office," he told her, gathering the material for the cast. "I tell the women to pretend they're from some exotic foreign country for three months."

Jenna thought she'd like to use the saw on Stan. Instead, she counted to ten. "Could we make an exception this time?"

He paused and looked at her. "How much does it bother you?"

"I would beg," Jenna said, "but I can't bend my leg to kneel."

Stan met her gaze and drummed his pen against his thigh. It struck Jenna that even though Stan wore a white coat and a tie, used the appropriate medical jargon with ease and oozed professional confidence, he didn't *look* like a doctor. His hair was slightly mussed, his shoulders broad like an athlete, his facial features roughly masculine. He was just too male, she thought. Too sexy.

Jenna blinked. For crying out loud, where had that thought come from?

Stan shrugged his shoulders. "Oh, what the hell. I've got a little extra time." He turned away and rummaged through a drawer, pulling out a disposable razor. After lathering her leg again, he lifted the razor.

Jenna stiffened, and blocked him with her hand. "I can do this."

Stan laughed. "Ha. That's funny. You shave your leg and cut yourself, get an infection, then sue me."

"I wouldn't sue you," she insisted.

He shook his head. "You have two choices, Jenna Jean. I shave or no shave."

If she thought she could possibly bear the stubble, she would have turned him down, but she couldn't. She should get past her qualms. After all, when Stan looked at her leg, he probably viewed it like a mechanic viewed machinery. He didn't look at her leg and think anything sexual. She took a breath. "Okay. You shave."

He nodded, then hesitated, looking as if he were fighting a smile.

"What?" Jenna asked.

"I'm just wondering what the guys on Cherry Lane would say if they could see me shaving Jenna Jean Anderson's leg."

Jenna scowled. "You mean *The Bad Boys Club*, that group of juvenile delinquent wannabes who terrorized our neighborhood."

Stan chuckled. "We were so proud of ourselves when Emily St. Clair's mother turned up her nose at us and called us *The Bad Boys Club*." He slowly swiped the razor from her ankle to her knee, making a path through the soapsuds to her bare skin. "A bunch of us swore we were going to get bad boy tattoos."

Jenna looked at him in disbelief. "You didn't."

His eyes turned mischievous. "Want me to show you?"

An illicit thrill ran through her at the expression on his face, and she quickly shook her head. "I don't believe it."

"We could only get our hands on permanent markers, and despite the claim,'' he said as he skimmed the razor over another area of skin, ''they aren't permanent.''

He was close enough for her to smell his aftershave and count each of his eyelashes. She could see the reminiscence flicker through his brown eyes. Feeling an odd, bumpy sensation in her stomach as he shaved her leg in long sensual strokes, she held her breath.

''Those guys were the closest thing to brothers I ever had,'' he murmured.

Jenna heard the faint longing in his voice and cocked her head to one side. ''Why don't you find some of them?''

He lifted his shoulder in a half shrug. ''I don't know. People don't always turn out the way you hope.'' He glanced up to meet her gaze. ''Unlike you. Everyone always knew Jenna Jean would be something important.''

Her heart twisted at the sincere compliment. ''Thank you, but I've got a ways to go.''

His glance swept over her body. ''You look like you've done pretty well to me.''

Her skin heated, but she willed herself not to blush. Despite the fact that she was clearly not at her best, Stan made her feel attractive, even sexy. Giving a quick tiny shake of her head, she wondered if it was possible for a broken leg to affect one's brain.

She cleared her throat. ''You're very good with that razor.''

He finished the job with one long swipe, then began to rinse her leg. ''I love my work,'' he told her with a wink.

''What do you love about it?''

"Humpty Dumpty complex. I like putting people back together again."

"After they've fallen apart," she said, her respect for him growing, her curiosity also growing. "How many legs do you shave?"

"For surgery?"

She shook her head.

"Ah, you mean for women with broken legs who can't bear unshaven legs." He shook his head. "None. You got special treatment."

"Because I'm a lawyer or because I used to beat you in one-on-one?"

"Neither. I've just always liked your legs."

Nearly helpless for the next two weeks, Jenna was forced to rely on help from her brothers and Maddie. She hated the cast and was impatient with the pain and her general weakness.

Dr. Stan Michaels was a continual surprise. Every time she saw him, he was both professional and sympathetic. Edgy from her boredom, she found his manner consistently reassuring.

Filling the hours and finding an outlet for her energy, however, was another matter. Accustomed to jogging three days a week, she deplored the inactivity. Her schedule barely allowed her time to breathe. Now she had too much time.

Too much time to think.

Too much time to think about how few people she allowed close to her. Part of her was chafing at the bit to get back to work, but part of her wanted something more. Perhaps it was the overdose of women's magazines, but with nothing to distract her, for the first time in years, Jenna took a hard look at what she'd pushed aside for her career.

Physically vulnerable, she became aware of a softer side to herself. It was as disconcerting and awkward as using crutches, because she'd focused on developing all the toughness she needed to succeed. In the quiet darkness of her house, however, there'd been many nights when the toughness felt like clothing that didn't fit right, and she had longed to hold and be held by someone.

She wondered what it would be like to have a man in her life. Not a husband, not necessarily a passionate lover, certainly no fantasy man, but a nice man whom she cared for and who cared for her. Someone with whom to share bits and pieces of their lives.

The notion drew her, lured her, and like a secret picture in a locket, it stayed with her all the time, even when she returned to work.

After she went back to work, the opportunity to discuss her dream of being a judge with her boss appeared like a gift. Carefully choosing her words, she revealed her goal to him. His response, however, wasn't what she'd dreamed.

"He laughed," Jenna said miserably at the end of the day to her two best friends, Emily Ramsey and Maddie Blackwell. Emily was visiting from North Carolina and the three women had been planning to get together for some time. Unfortunately, Jenna had just had one of the worst days of her life, and her leg ached. "The commonwealth attorney laughed when I told him I wanted to be a judge."

Emily winced.

Maddie scowled. "Did you kick him?"

She had wanted to wrap his tongue around his throat. Jenna glanced down at her cast. "Kicking would have been difficult."

"Do you want me to beat him up for you?"

Maddie's comment drew a reluctant smile. She had made the same offer to both her friends at various times. "He's an attorney. He would slap you with assault so fast it would make your head spin."

Emily sighed. "Well, did he say anything positive? Anything at all?"

"He said I was a born prosecutor, and I have an overly developed sense of fair play that would make it politically difficult for me to become a judge. You see," she said, "the local bar recommends the candidates."

"And you've beaten the heck out of all of them in court," Emily said.

"Not all," Jenna corrected. "But maybe I didn't cut as many deals as I should."

"Would you have felt right cutting more deals?"

Jenna felt a sinking sensation. "No." She paused. "But I still want to be a judge."

"And you still can," Maddie said. "It just might take a little longer to get there. In the meantime," she began.

Jenna didn't wonder what would come next. After being married for a year now, Maddie had decided it was time for Jenna to get married, too.

"You can devote some attention to other areas of your life."

"Basketball's out for now," Jenna muttered and took another drink of her screwdriver. She wondered why Emily was eating Saltine crackers nonstop.

Maddie smiled in a deceptively sweet way. "I tried to say this nicely, but you force me to be blunt. You need to get a life. A social life. A personal life."

"A man," Emily added, surprising Jenna with her candor. Although Emily had come into her own in a major way during the past two years, she was the only polite one in the bunch.

Restless, Jenna grabbed her crutches and rose from the sofa. Usually she stopped this discussion before it was out of the gate, but she'd had her dreams smashed today and two screwdrivers to loosen her tongue. "I don't do well with men in social settings. My mother says it's because I'm always trying to one-up them. She says I should be more demure. I think she thinks I should conceal my intelligence."

Emily crunched another cracker and shook her head. "A woman conceals flabby thighs, not her intelligence."

"You just haven't met the right man," Maddie said. "The right man will love your intelligence and everything else about you. He'll even be able to deal with how controlling you are."

"You've been reading those fairy tales at bedtime again, haven't you?" Jenna said, hobbling across her carpet.

"I speak from experience."

"Same here," Emily said.

Jenna sighed. "You met extraordinary men, the only two extraordinary men on this planet. Now there are none left."

Jenna saw the gleam in Maddie's eye, and if she'd been a little less crushed or a little less smashed, she would have put up her guard.

"I think you should meet one of my customers," Maddie said, and Jenna immediately groaned. Maddie worked as a travel agent and met the oddest assortment of people possible.

"He's very well educated, good-looking and lonely."

"Have you suggested a kitten to him?"

"Jenna Jean," Maddie said in an indignant voice.

"Jenna," she corrected and sighed again. She thought of how much she'd devoted to her career and the community during the past several years. She'd never been good with men socially. She'd successfully avoided the issue of dating for most of her life. The past two weeks had afforded her lots of time to think. Time to think about the fact that her life was out of balance. Maybe it was time for a change.

"Well educated and good-looking." She immediately thought of Stan Michaels and his memorable voice. Much to her dismay, she had thought about him more than once over the past couple of weeks. "What is his voice like?"

Maddie glanced at her sideways and shrugged. "He's no Pavarotti, but it's okay."

Okay. Jenna didn't want okay. She wanted a man with a great speaking voice, who was bright and had a good heart. She swore under her breath. Perhaps this could be a first step to achieving some balance in her life. "I promised to attend a fund-raiser next week—"

"I'll give him your phone number."

And Jenna wondered why she felt like she'd just put her neck under the guillotine.

Three

He was well educated. He was attractive.

But Jenna couldn't get past the fact that he had a voice like Kermit the Frog.

His beeper rescued her. Or rescued him, depending on one's point of view. Midway through the fund-raiser, he had to leave, and Jenna's ankle began to throb. Men had cut out on her for many reasons, but this one took the cake. Her date was a scientist, and his ant farm had gotten loose.

"You've been on your feet too long," a familiar male voice said from behind her.

She whipped around and wobbled, instantly frustrated by her unsteadiness. She glanced up into Dr. Stanley Michaels's intent, all-seeing gaze. "No, I haven't," she automatically denied.

"When did it start hurting?"

She opened her mouth to deny it again, then shrugged. "Only about five minutes ago."

He put his hand at the small of her back and nodded to the side of the room. "There's a straight chair that has your name on it. What are you doing here?"

Jenna didn't feel like objecting, so she hobbled forward and sat down. "The Youth League is one of my pet causes, and they invited me to the fund-raiser a long time ago." She watched him prop her crutches against the wall. He wore his dark suit with ease. He would, she thought, wear any clothes with ease. She'd bet he would be at ease naked, too.

Jenna widened her eyes at herself. For Pete's sake, where had that thought come from? Testosterone overload, she concluded. Stan Michaels was one of those men who oozed sex. Too primitive for her taste. "You're in civilian clothes, tonight. Why are you here? I seem to recall you had a few brushes with the law. Are you here to give a turn-around testimonial?"

He gave her a wry glance. "Maybe another time. Tonight, I'm here to—"

"To?" she prompted.

He stuffed his hands in his suit pockets. "Get involved in the community."

Jenna blinked at the flash of vulnerability that deepened his eyes for a millisecond. "Pardon?"

He looked self-conscious and slightly irritated at the same time. "C'mon, Jenna Jean, you've never been one to miss much. You heard me the first time."

Jenna paused. Stan was keeping her on her toes. She was caught between her experiences with him when they'd been much younger and who he was today. The man he had become, she sensed, had a greater depth and was searching for something. The knowledge nudged at her.

"Are you interested in throwing money around or doing something?"

His gaze met hers. "Both."

"The Youth League has a program set up where they arrange basketball games for inner-city youth once a week. They're *always* looking for more men."

"I'll keep it in mind," he said, and the corners of his eyes crinkled in a sexually teasing way. "What about you? I notice the guy who was hanging around you earlier is gone. Are you looking for another man?"

"Only one who drives a Yellow Cab," Jenna muttered and fought a tinge of embarrassment. She wasn't sure how much to reveal. "He was paged and had to leave."

"Heavy date?"

She shook her head. She was *not* going to tell him it was a blind date. "Just friends."

"Blind date, huh?"

Jenna stifled an oath and stood. "My ankle feels better. I think I'll get a drink." She grabbed her crutches and quickly hobbled toward the bar. In her rush she snagged a crutch on one of the legs of the table holding hors d'oeuvres and pitched forward. Swearing, she fell helplessly toward the floor until an arm fastened around her waist and she was jerked backward.

Her back plastered intimately against the well-muscled frame of Stan Michaels, she struggled for breath.

"If you wanted a drink that much, I could have gotten it for you," Stan muttered against her ear.

A terrible, wicked, totally unacceptable thrill raced through her. "I was trying to get away from you," she retorted.

He chuckled. "You need to chill, Jenna Jean. You could have ended up face first on the floor. Worse yet, you could have reinjured your ankle."

"Jenna," she corrected and gathered her wits. "Thank you." Distressed at the way her heart was racing, she made a sound of frustration. "Could you please help me get the crutches?"

"Sure," he said, and bent down to grab first one, then the other.

She noticed the calm, capable way he helped her. His hands were sculpted, yet strong looking. She took a breath and smelled his aftershave mixed with his masculine scent. His gaze met hers, and her stomach dipped in an odd way. The sensation confused her.

"Thank you," she managed, and realized they were standing too close. That was the problem, she decided, and started to move backward.

His hands shot out to steady her. "Whoa! There are two little old ladies with martinis right behind you."

"Oh." Jenna prayed he would take his hands off her and cleared her throat. "Thank you, again."

His eyes were serious. "You really need to be careful about putting weight on that ankle. It's still early days."

"I'll do better," she promised, and wiggled her arms in a hint for him to release her. He did, and she drew a breath of relief.

"I understand you saw my associate last week," he said.

"That's right." She nodded. "They said you were in surgery."

"Miss me?" he asked in a semisexy, almost-flirting voice.

Jenna didn't blink before she responded. Dr. Stan Michaels was a little too charming, smooth and sure of himself.

"No," she said, and was extremely proud that she restrained herself from clubbing him with her crutch when he laughed.

"Stan!" a voice from the past called, interrupting his observation of Jenna Jean as she left him eating her dust. Well, he modified, that was her intent. Her broken leg kept her from moving too fast.

He looked toward his school chum and shook his head. "Eddie Ridenhour, it's been years."

Eddie thrust out his hand. "Yep, and I hear you're a doctor now. Surprised the heck out of me."

Stan chuckled. "I won't ask what you meant by that. You and I spent too many hours in detention. You know my secrets. What about you?"

"I run a car dealership." He whipped out a business card. "If you need a car, I'm your man. My wife's into all this charity stuff. I come to these things for the free eats and potential customers. Every once in a while I donate transportation for one of their activities. So, why're you here? Looking for women?"

"Free eats," Stan said blandly. "You got kids?"

Eddie wore a pained expression. "Have I got

kids?'' He pulled out his wallet and released a plastic-covered cascade of pictures. ''Try six of them.''

Stan listened to the woes of parenthood for the next several minutes and caught sight of Jenna on the other side of the room. She was leaning against the wall as if it were her date. She was prettier and tougher than she used to be, he mused, and she'd never been a softy.

Eddie followed his gaze. ''Ah, you've already found Jenna the Knife. Now, that's a scary woman.''

''Scary?''

''She can shred a defendant at thirty paces.''

Stan shrugged. ''Isn't that her job?''

''Yeah, I guess so. I just hear she's a rule follower to the max.''

''What's she like socially?''

''I don't know. My wife might, though. My guess is most of her social stuff is wrapped around her job. She's no slouch. I hear she helped put three of her brothers through college.''

''Busy lady,'' Stan said thoughtfully.

''Great rear end,'' Eddie said, then shook his head. ''I just can't get past the nickname. It reminds me of Lorena Bobbit, you know, that woman who cut off her husband's—''

Stan chuckled. ''I don't think she's seeing anyone.''

''Probably not. You interested?''

Stan watched Jenna swirl her finger in her drink, then bring it to her lips to suck it. The sensual gesture was at odds with her controlled demeanor. It made him wonder what else was beneath the surface.

''Hey, Stan, you interested?''

"Curious," he said.

"Well, listen, my wife is friends with this great blonde. Her name's Tina, and she's been hounding me for an introduction all evening. You don't mind meeting her, do you?"

Stan sighed, glancing in Jenna's direction. "No. I don't mind."

"Wanna ride?" Stan asked Jenna as she lifted the phone in the hotel lobby.

She hesitated. "I was just going to call a cab."

"I'm cheaper," he said, and glanced out the glass doors. "And it's raining."

"I don't usually mind the rain, but I was told to keep the cast dry." Her eyes glinted with humor, and she dipped her head. "Thanks for the offer."

He gave the valet his keys, and they waited for his car. "Successful evening?" he asked.

"Somewhat," Jenna said, leaning her back against the outside wall of the hotel and closing her eyes. He suspected Jenna wasn't much of a leaner. Since she was still active and athletic, she probably resented the hell out of the restrictions her broken ankle placed on her.

He took a moment to look at her. Her silky dark hair was cut in a classic, shoulder-length pageboy that would require a very determined man to mess it up. His fingers itched, and he stuffed them in his pockets. She wore a black suit that would go from court to cocktail party. The modest cut of the suit didn't completely conceal her feminine curves. No jewelry except a super-slim gold watch and pearl earrings.

She clearly cultivated a don't-touch-me air. It was

almost as if it were stamped on her like an unbreakable rule.

Which made Stan want to release the buttons of her jacket and find out what was underneath. He glanced back at her face and decided she looked tired enough to fall asleep propped against the wall. "Somewhat," he prompted.

She sighed. "I didn't get away completely unscathed. I got roped into helping plan an event at Smith Mountain Lake."

"The weekend after July Fourth?"

She opened her eyes. "Yes."

"Did Mitzi ask you?"

Her blue gaze grew wary. "Yes, why?"

"She bagged me, too."

"Uh-oh." She smiled slightly. "Well, I guess you're involved now."

The valet eased his Lexus forward and opened the door.

"Very nice," she said with approval as he helped her in to the car. "I'm surprised you left the party alone."

"Why?" Stan asked as he slid behind the wheel.

"That blonde looked like she was hoping to permanently attach herself to your shoulder."

Stan grinned. Jenna didn't sound envious. Just curious, like him. "Tina," Stan said. "Eddie introduced her. She's a friend of his wife's. Not really my type." He accelerated forward. "Where am I going?" he asked.

"Southwest, toward Crystal Creek. I live on Laburnum."

"Far from Cherry Lane?"

He felt her gaze on him. "Not too far," she said. "It's a quiet, settled neighborhood, but there are some kids. I'm sure there are some girls who play princess and boys who try to steal cookies." She paused. "What made you come back?"

"I didn't find what I was looking for in those other places. I didn't find what I needed," he admitted. "I'm hoping I can find it here. What made you come back to Roanoke right after law school?"

He saw her shrug out of the corner of his eye. "It was home, where I wanted to make a difference. My brothers have always driven me crazy, but I felt responsible to help them if I could." She laughed softly to herself. "My personal contribution to reducing the number of juvenile delinquents on the street."

"Why not private practice?"

She sighed. "Because I have a terrible flaw," she confessed in a low voice.

The sound caressed his nerve endings the same way a confession of her sensual secrets might. "What's that?"

"I have an overdeveloped sense of fairness," she replied with disgust.

"I guess that could be a problem for a lawyer."

"Don't besmirch my profession. It is a problem, a terrible problem. It could even keep me from reaching a professional goal."

Stan shot a quick glance at her and saw that she was serious. He had thought she was kidding. "Fairness is a great quality."

"It's immature."

"Shows character."

"Idealistic, pie-in-the-sky."

"A good ideal," he corrected, "which makes a person better than he thought he could be."

She stopped and he felt her stare at him. "You know, you keep surprising me. Every time I think I've got you pegged, you—"

He grinned at her baffled tone. "I what?"

"You change," she said. "When we were younger, I didn't think you were much concerned about character, or fairness, for that matter."

"I wasn't."

"You were out for lots of laughs and a good time."

"That's right."

"So when did you change?"

He thought about hedging. It was a personal subject for him, and he could tell Jenna wasn't totally sympathetic. He grappled with it for a moment, then remembered that change wasn't always comfortable. "There was a guy who became a doctor. He was smart, well liked. He enjoyed a good time. He might not have been a brilliant doctor, but he was a very good one."

"Like you?"

He grinned. "Is this your gentle way of suggesting I'm not brilliant?"

"I'm sure you know," she told him, "that brilliance isn't all it's cracked up to be."

"You would know?"

"I didn't say that."

He chuckled. "Uh-huh."

"Please go on. This is the most interesting conversation I've had all night."

"I'm not forgetting the 'brilliant' comment."

"He was a very good doctor," she said.

"Yes. Committed to his career and a good time."

"Not married."

"Right."

"No kids."

Stan nodded. "None, and no driving causes."

"Okay. I'm lost. What does this have to do with you coming back to Roanoke?"

"He got sick, and within a year he died." Stan took a deep breath, recalling the way Chuck's friends had scattered during that last year. "Three people attended his funeral. He was the same age as me, and he didn't leave anything behind. It's almost like he didn't exist."

A thoughtful silence settled between them. It wasn't uncomfortable, Stan noticed. There was too much energy for discomfort. He could sense it in Jenna, in himself.

"I think you might be wrong about your friend," she finally said. "He left behind at least three people who cared about him. And," she added, "he obviously made an impression on you."

He braked for a stoplight and was surprised at the way her words eased him. He met her gaze, seeing sincerity, intelligence. And passion. The combination got his attention like an elbow in the ribs. Even with her sharp tongue, the Knife had heart.

From the light of a streetlamp, Stan took a second and third look at Jenna's face. Although she was attractive, she wasn't the prettiest woman he'd ever met. But she had blue eyes that could slice a man in half one moment and deepen with compassion in a flash. She was more substance than style. Until a few months ago he would have considered her too complex, too intense, too much.

He still did, he told himself, and he should resist the crazy urge to muss her hair, snap her bra strap and generally rattle her cage. The last time he'd followed unbidden urges for Jenna Jean, she'd nearly bitten his hand off.

She was staring at him with the same force he was staring at her, though, and Stan was certain the energy between them could have zapped all the mosquitoes east of the Mississippi. Against his better judgment, he lifted his finger to her chin, then skimmed it up to her mouth.

He watched her eyes widen. "You're very good," he said. "I wonder if you still bite."

She was thinking about it. Her eyes flashed, and she opened her mouth, then seemed to reconsider and pulled back. "In the mood for a little S&M?" she asked in a smoky voice. "You'll have to get that somewhere else."

Stan laughed and accelerated.

"You're going too fast," she told him as he pulled into her neighborhood.

"No problem. I've got the assistant commonwealth attorney riding with me."

"All the more reason," she began.

"To drive like my Great-Aunt Martha," he finished. "She always stays ten miles below the speed limit."

"It looks like you still have a need to break the rules," she said. "Take the next left. My house is the third one on the right."

He checked to see if she was looking down her

nose at him. Almost. He smothered a grin. "That's a generalization, and generalizations are often specifically inaccurate." He pulled up her driveway. "I believe in rules."

"Is that so?" Her voice oozed skepticism.

"They're just different rules than yours. For example," he continued as he stopped the car, "kissing. I bet you have rules about kissing."

Jenna shifted slightly, then seemed to catch herself. "Maybe," she said, then shrugged. "Yes, I have a few rules about kissing. I try not to kiss anyone I don't like. I'm interested in quality over quantity. My previous impressions of you indicate you were interested in quantity."

Stan grinned. She was so snooty. He felt like he was twelve years old again, wanting to teach Jenna Jean a thing or two. "You're right about one thing. I don't have rules about quantity."

"But I do have a rule for kissing." He lowered his mouth closer to hers. "Never kiss for less than thirty seconds."

Four

Jenna should tell him.

She should tell Stan not to waste his time. After all, she'd been told she was a boring kisser. She should, but for some reason, she didn't want to.

Stan looked at her mouth, then his gaze slowly climbed to meet hers. His brown eyes held a wicked glint of challenge. Jenna's heart slammed against her rib cage. She felt suddenly, inexplicably light-headed.

Her defenses finally kicked into action, and she backed up nearly to the door. "You're crazy."

"I've never denied it," he said in a melting voice as he moved closer to her.

"Insane," she added breathlessly, staring at him.

"Possibly."

"Looney Tunes." He was *way* too close, and she was too aware of his body. She could feel his breath on her face, smell his scent, and her always-clear head felt like it was filled with mud.

"Probably. C'mon, Jenna Jean, it's only thirty seconds," he muttered, his mouth almost, but not quite brushing hers.

"Ummm..." She noticed the shape of his lips and wondered just what kind of kisser Saint Stan was. Her mind and body buzzed with curiosity. A forbidden excitement raced through her. "I—uh—"

"If you're going to say no, say it now."

The arousal in his eyes made her chest feel tight. "I—"

She didn't say it fast enough. His mouth took hers, and Jenna widened her eyes. *What was she doing kissing Stanley Michaels?*

Shock rendered her motionless, but she felt every move he made. His chest barely brushed her breasts, but he didn't touch her with his hands or hold her in his arms. He only held her with his mouth. And there was something incredibly erotic about the way he tilted his mouth from side to side, exploring her lips.

Gentle persuasion. Something deep inside her eased and said she could trust him. He nibbled at her bottom lip, coaxing. He wanted her response, and would take his time to get it. She could feel his checked desire rolling through him, flowing into her.

Her heart beat faster, her objections faded, she sighed, and he sipped the soft breath from her lips. She felt the pull of pleasure and an odd dissatisfaction. She couldn't say what she wanted, but she knew it was more.

She opened her mouth, meeting his unspoken challenge, his sensual invitation. His low groan tugged at her, deep in her stomach. Sensation won over thought, and she sank into the kiss.

She echoed his movements, pressing, rubbing, sucking. He teased her with his tongue, darting it out to taste her lips, then pulling back. His mouth consumed her attention, but she was peripherally aware of heat. She was hot. The tips of her breasts were tight, and she wondered how the pressure of his body against hers would feel.

Frustration made her bold, and she opened her mouth wider. She slid her tongue past his lips and his gentle persuasion went up in smoke. His chest meshed with hers, he thrust his tongue into her mouth, and she sucked it in response.

An erotic image pulsed through her mind and blood, of her body naked and tangled with his, of him sliding inside her like his tongue. Sinking, she reached for his shoulders.

As soon as she touched him, he pulled back and swore under his breath.

Thankful the door window supported her head, she stared at him and tried to come to the surface. Her body was thrumming with arousal, her brain clouded. She sucked in several mind-clearing breaths and searched for something to say.

"I need to go in," she finally managed. *I need to get away from you.* She fumbled with the doorknob. *I need a brain transplant. I've just let Stanley Michaels kiss me, and I liked it.*

Alarm shot through her, and she opened the door.

"Wait a minute," he said.

"A minute? No way. Look what thirty seconds did," she muttered, and swung her legs out the door.

If she had to crawl, she was going to get to her front door. She reached for the crutches in the back seat, and Stan grabbed them from his side of the car.

Stan swore again and was at her door within seconds. "You have got to be the most independent, determined woman I have met in my life. Do you *ever* ask for help?"

"As a general rule, no," she told him, hobbling toward her porch.

"We're going to have to do something about your rules."

She rebelled at the suggestion. "My rules have worked just fine for me. There's no—" She broke off when he set her crutches down on the walkway.

"What are you doing?" she asked inanely as he wrapped his arms around her and carried her up the steps. The last man who'd carried her had been her father, and that had been about twenty years ago.

"It's late," he said. "This is faster and easier. Where's your key?"

Her instinct was to argue, but she sensed it would just prolong his presence. She dug the key out of her purse, and he shifted her so she could push it into the lock and turn it. He shoved the door open with his shoulder and set her down on the sofa, then retrieved her crutches.

He joined her on the sofa and looked at her. His expression held too many layers of emotion for her to read them all.

She swallowed. "You're not going to kiss me again."

"Not tonight," he agreed. "You're making me

change my rules, Jenna Jean. Thirty seconds isn't nearly long enough with you.''

"Okay," Maddie said, sipping mimosa at Emily's mother's well-appointed home as she wrote. "We're making a list. Great voice, intelligent, not intimidated by intelligent women."

Jenna had learned that with Maddie, if you opened the door just a crack, she would blow it the rest of the way off the hinges. "I'm not sure this is a good idea," she told her, and knew she might as well try to stop a speeding train. "I just said I was going to start dating and have more of a social life."

"This is a great idea. I'll make copies of the list for Emily and her mother, so they can keep an eye out for a few good men."

"This is beginning to sound like a recruiting commercial for the marines," Jenna muttered, noting that Emily was eating Saltine crackers again. Her leg itched inside her cast, and she wished she'd brought the little plastic lawn rake. Stan had recommended it and warned her not to use a coat hanger. She'd seen him once since he'd kissed the stuffing out of her, and he'd been purely professional at her doctor appointment.

He'd probably forgotten about that mind-blowing thirty seconds, and that was for the best, she told herself. However, she felt a sizable twinge of disappointment. It was just female pride, she rationalized, that she wished he'd been at least as affected as she had been.

"Jenna Jean, for the third time, what else do you want in a man?"

"Jenna," she corrected Maddie, and shrugged. "I don't know. That's such a general question. I'd like him to be—clean."

Emily laughed.

Maddie rolled her eyes. "You're such help. What do you want him to look like? Tall, medium. Is face more important than body? What kind of personality? What—"

"Taller than I am," Jenna said. "Normal body. I don't want someone who's competing for Mr. America. Not too fat or too thin. It would be nice if his face was attractive. Brown eyes," she murmured, thinking of Stan. "I like it when men will look me in the eye and—" She broke off when it hit her she was describing Stan.

"Now we're getting somewhere. Brown eyes—"

Flustered, Jenna shook her head. "No, it doesn't have to be brown eyes."

"But you just said—"

Jenna stood. "I know, but I didn't really mean it that way. He just needs to have—eyes—"

Maddie's gaze widened. "Okeydoke. I think we can probably find a man with eyes."

Embarrassed, Jenna realized how much she'd thought of Stan. It irritated her. He wasn't right for her. He was just playing with her. He— *There she went again.* She sighed in exasperation. "I'm more concerned with personality. He needs to be a reasonable man, someone who won't expect me to be at his beck and call. He won't pressure me for marriage or kids. He won't be arrogant or a flirt," she continued, naming everything that Stan *wasn't*.

Maddie and Emily looked at each other, then back

at Jenna. "Are you sure you want a man in your life?" Emily asked. "They can be more messy than puppies."

"Emily," Maddie said in a warning voice.

"I'm serious. Marriage isn't for everyone. Maybe Jenna would be happier with a dog."

Jenna stared at Emily. "Are you having problems with Beau?"

"Not really, but—"

"Not really!" Maddie repeated in alarm.

Emily sighed. "Ignore me. I'm in a weird mood."

Jenna watched Emily glumly munch another cracker and sip lemonade. A suspicion came to mind. "Have you told him you're pregnant yet?"

Emily's eyes widened. Maddie squealed. Then Emily burst into tears, and Jenna rushed to her side.

"He said he wanted to wait another year, b-b-but I had to go off the Pill and one night we forgot until it was t-too—"

"Late," Jenna finished for her, her own eyes watering at the anguish in Emily's voice.

"He's worried about money because my parents have a lot and he doesn't, but I don't care about—" Her voice broke, and her pretty face crumpled. "I'm so scared."

Maddie wrapped her arm around Emily's shoulder. "Oh, Emily, Emily. You've got to tell him."

Jenna nodded. "She's right. You can't do this by yourself. Do you really think he would want you to?"

"I don't know. We were so happy, and I'm excited about the baby, but I don't know how he'll feel about it."

"Where is he right now?" Jenna asked.

Emily looked appalled. "I can't tell him now. He's on the golf course with my stepfather. My mother and I are supposed to meet them for dinner at the country club."

"The later you wait," Jenna began.

"The more majorly ticked off he's gonna be," Maddie finished. "Joshua would blow a gasket if I didn't tell him the second I knew."

"It's getting more difficult to hide the morning sickness," Emily admitted. "And he doesn't understand why I haven't wanted to ride his horse or the new motorcycle I begged him to get."

"Motorcycle?" Jenna echoed, then shook her head. "Don't explain. What you need is a plan," Jenna told her, much more comfortable that the attention was off her for the moment. "Instead of eating dinner with your parents, you should get him alone…"

She continued, with Maddie's input, to help Emily plan. By the time they finished, Emily was still a little shaky, but she looked resolved.

"There, that's settled," Maddie agreed. She took a last sip of mimosa and nodded, then twirled the pencil in her fingers.

Jenna felt a sinking sensation in her stomach. Maddie had a determined glint in her eye. If Jenna hadn't played princess with Maddie twenty years ago, she could have told her to take a hike. Instead, she would have to endure.

Maddie smiled. "Okay, Jenna Jean, I haven't forgotten you. Back to the list."

Jenna poured herself another mimosa and let it rip. Might as well get it over with. "I want a man who will adore me, worship the ground I walk on and kiss me until I forget my name.'' *Take that, Stanley Michaels.*

She grinned at Maddie's gaping expression. ''It would be nice if he liked the water and didn't eat food off my plate or snitch my cookies without my permission. I want a man with a good heart and a bad imagination, but he's got to be controllable.''

Emily swallowed her Saltine and shook her head. ''I still think we should get her a dog.''

Stan slid into a seat in the back of the courtroom. Jenna Jean had been busy; too busy to return his calls the past two days. He needed to talk with her about the Youth League Day at the lake. That was it, he told himself.

Jenna Jean wasn't his type.

He was curious as hell about her. She dressed more conservatively than his mother, but kissed with enough heat to melt the polar icecaps. That didn't, however, change the fact that she wasn't his type.

Stan watched her approach the bench on crutches. He would lay odds that she cursed that cast with every other breath. She counted on her quickness and agility. Stan should know. This was the same girl with whom he'd raced and run through sprinklers. Until he had his growth spurt, she'd won too many times to count. He'd always had to try a little more, run a little faster, work a little harder when he'd competed with Jenna Jean.

Her energy was in check today behind a navy suit, with a red silk square in her breast pocket and a white blouse. Slacks covered her legs and the cast. Her dark hair was pulled into a knot at the base of her neck.

All business, he thought, and wondered why she still looked feminine to him. She spoke in a low voice to the judge, then turned her attention to the witness.

She started out nice and easy, polite and agreeable. She didn't smile, but her voice was warm, and she nodded. Invoking trust, she gave the impression of being everybody's most dependable sister.

So why was her competence so sexy to him? And why was he mentally stripping the navy suit from her? Why was he thinking about her heat, when she looked so cool?

Leaning back in his seat, he watched her build on the trust, then slice the defendant to ribbons. It was the guy's third DUI. He would be thumbing or riding his bike to the office for a long while.

The judge pounded the gavel, and Stan rose as court was adjourned. He watched Jenna shake hands with the other attorney, pull her briefcase strap over her shoulder and make her way toward the back of the room.

When she caught sight of him, her eyes widened in surprise, then wariness. She looked confused. "I didn't see your name on a list. Did you already run a red light, or are you fighting a speeding ticket, or—"

Stan chuckled. "No, Jenna. I haven't been charged with anything."

She looked at him blankly. "Oh," she said, "then why are you here?"

He shrugged and walked alongside her. "I'm here to see you." When she flicked another wary glance at him, he tossed back an innocent look and added, "About the Youth League Day at the lake."

"Why?"

"We need to do some planning, and I wanted your input on using motor skis. Let's eat lunch."

She began to shake her head. "I don't have ti—"

"You gotta eat. This won't take long."

"I have too much to—"

"There's a little place across the street, and I'll buy. Here, let me—" After a mild struggle, he took her briefcase. "Did Webster put your name beside *stubborn* in the dictionary?"

"No, *determined*. He put yours beside *pushy*, though, didn't he?"

"Actually, I'm referenced in several entries. *Charming, handsome, brilliant*—"

"*Egotistical.*"

"*Confident*," he corrected, and grinned as he opened the door and they walked outside. It was a sunny, hot day, and the deli wasn't far. "It was fun seeing the Knife at work. I don't think the defendant expected you to go for the full sentence."

"He should have. I warned his attorney. The Ayatollah takes a hard line on repeat DUIs."

"Ayatollah?"

"Pet name for the commonwealth attorney," she said with a sugary smile and waved at someone who called out her name.

"Does he want Virginia to require a special license plate for repeat offenders?"

Jenna nodded. "Yes, and for people who still won't learn, I think a tattoo on the forehead is a good idea."

Stan grinned, but he agreed. "Sounds like the Ayatollah isn't the only one who takes a hard line. Here we are," he said, pointing to the deli.

"One good thing about my crutches," Jenna told him, "is how quickly I get a seat."

She was right. Although the deli was crowded, within a minute they were seated at a table. Soon after their drinks arrived.

"How much do you hate the cast?" Stan asked.

She slipped a finger in her carbonated fruit drink and swirled it around, then leaned closer to him as if she were sharing a confidence. "I fantasize about chain saws."

He watched her lift her finger to her mouth and discreetly taste it. He felt a tug deep in his gut and wondered why his tie suddenly felt tight. "I'm not surprised." He cleared his throat. "Is your drink okay?"

She glanced down at her glass and her finger. A sheepish expression flashed across her face. "I have difficulty keeping my fingers out of my drinks. I like to play in them. It's a problem at formal dinners. Excuse me," she murmured, and reached for her napkin.

"It's okay. No formal dinner here," he told her, wanting another glimpse of the less uptight Jenna. Too late, he saw, when she straightened her shoulders.

"What did you want to discuss about the Youth League Day?"

"I have a friend who will donate the use of his boat, ski equipment, and jet skis. Do we need to be concerned with liability?"

"Yes. I'll give Mitzi a release the kids can get signed." She shook her head. "It's a shame, though. Some of those kids will have a hard time nailing down their parents long enough to get a signature."

"Is there that much of a problem here?" Stan

asked, remembering how attentive his parents had been during his growing-up years.

"It can be. It's a sad fact, but there are more claims of neglect and abuse, and the solutions don't usually come easily. That's why most of the lawyers in the CA's office don't love Juvenile and Domestic Relations Court. It's hard to find an answer, let alone find a winner."

"But the Youth League is one of your pet causes?"

She nodded and reached for her glass, stopping herself before she put her finger in it again. "I think it's because it's so hard to do something about it in my profession. I get frustrated and need to feel like I'm doing something."

Stan saw the passion in her eyes again. He cocked his head to one side, wondering if a man could bring that look to her face, as well. He suspected lighting Jenna's passion would be a mind-blowing, rewarding but demanding proposition. He suspected a man would have to be nearly insane to try it, which showed he had a self-destructive streak, because he was tempted as hell.

He gently tugged a strand of her hair. "How many white hats do you have in your closet?"

She gave a grudging smile. "None. How many black hats do you have?"

Stan chuckled and shook his head. "You've got me all wrong, Jenna Jean. I'm the salt of the earth. They call me Saint Stan."

"Uh-huh," she said, the husky sound one of disbelief.

An idea came to him, one that had been brewing

in his mind throughout their conversation. "You should let me disprove your perception of me."

"Why?"

"Because in America a man is innocent until proven guilty."

"True, so how do you plan to prove your, uh, innocence?" she asked, nearly choking over the last word and gazing at him in confusion when he took her hand.

"I'm taking you for a ride on Sunday."

She paused, blinking. "Pardon?"

"A boat ride. We can kill two birds with one stone. Test my friend's yacht for Youth League Day, and let you see what a nice guy I am."

"Why do we need to test the boat? And what good would I be with this cast on my leg? And—"

He lifted her hand to his mouth and gently closed his teeth on her finger. He smiled at the way her eyes widened. "Relax, Jenna, you're not in court. You don't have to cross-examine. I'll bring your favorite drink. You sit back and ride on the boat for a while. Then you give your stamp of approval."

She looked so thoroughly, deliciously confused that he wanted to kiss her, but he'd already decided he wanted more than thirty seconds the next time.

"My stamp of approval on the boat?"

"Yeah, and me."

A hint of sexual awareness flittered through her gaze. She removed her hand from his. "I don't know about that, Saint Stan. Nice guys don't bite."

"Oh, yeah," he said, responding to the challenge rising inside him. He leaned closer and displayed the scar on his hand to give her a playful reminder. "Does that mean nice girls don't bite, either?"

It was crazy, but it was like an intimate secret between them. He watched her struggle with the memory and the electricity between them now. She touched his hand, then met his gaze. "Why should I go with you?"

"Because you're at least half as curious about me as I am about you."

Five

Jenna Jean had turned him down flat.

After she'd caught her breath.

She'd quickly masked the startled how-did-you-know-what-I-was-thinking look on her face, but Stan had seen it, and it had the same effect as an enticing flash of lace underwear.

To say the least, Jenna had a stimulating effect on him. It was more than sexual, different than he'd experienced before and he was growing more and more determined to understand it and her.

He wasn't done with her yet, he thought as he locked his car and walked toward his apartment. He noticed the same kid was shooting hoops again. More often than not, Stan found him on the community blacktop, but he'd never seen the kid's parents. The boy was such a loner that Stan had begun to wonder about his background. Stan had sublet an apartment in the complex on a temporary basis until he decided where to buy a house. Most of the apartment residents were busy, young, single people or a few young, married couples with very young children.

The boy didn't fit the demographics. He looked about thirteen, with longer hair, a faded T-shirt and worn denim shorts. Although the tenants weren't affluent, most appeared well on their way. Something about this boy reminded him of one of his childhood friends. The similarity was like a pinch that didn't stop. Curious, Stan loosened his tie and tucked it in his pocket, then jumped up to catch a rebound.

"Would you shoot a few with an older guy?"

The boy gave him a long, assessing look, then shrugged. He was clearly not the type to trust easily. "Okay."

"Stan."

"Jordan."

"Thirty," Stan added.

"Old enough," Jordan said. "You're wasting the daylight."

Lifting his eyebrows at the boy's attitude, Stan dribbled down and planned his lay-up. He dodged and feinted, then shot. And missed. Jordan grabbed the ball.

"How old's old enough?"

"Almost fourteen. I can take care of myself," Jordan said, then dribbled past Stan and shot the ball. And made it.

Stan grinned and snagged the rebound. "You're good on the court. I see you out here all the time. Which building do your parents live in?"

"My parents are dead," he said in a matter-of-fact voice. "I live with my brother."

"Oh, really," Stan said in a casual voice. "How old is he?"

With eyes far too old for a kid so young, Jordan met his gaze. "Old enough."

Over the next couple of days, Stan spent some time with Jordan and fed him some bachelor dinners. Food loosened the kid's tongue, and Stan learned that when he'd said "old enough" about his older brother, he'd meant twenty-two. He also learned that Jordan didn't live in the apartments where he spent so much time playing basketball. The apartments where he lived housed a rougher, noisier group of people, and it wasn't unusual to see an argument that turned physical and hear shots fired or a police siren. Jordan preferred a quieter environment so much that he rode a few miles on his bike every day to reach it.

When Stan asked Jordan what his brother's job was, he shrugged his shoulders and said, "Depends on the week." It shouldn't have bothered him for more than a moment. After all, Jordan was no relation to him. He was just a transient kid who happened to play basketball outside his back door...a kid with too-old eyes who reminded Stan of someone from his childhood.

Sunday afternoon, Stan was up for the hunt and capture of one female attorney, Miss Jenna Jean Anderson. As he pulled into her driveway, he was betting he would catch her doing near nothing. He wondered what it would take to catch her *wearing* near nothing. The thought teased him.

He rang her doorbell and heard her hobble to answer the door. At first glance a guilty look crossed her face.

Stan grinned. "Hi. Just thought I'd buzz by to see if you were busy. Looks like you're not, so—"

"I am," Jenna quickly said. "I'm busy."

Stan raised his eyebrows. "Oh, yeah. What are you doing?"

"I'm—" She hesitated, then released a drawn-out sigh. "I'm baking cookies."

"Great!" Stan pushed the door the rest of the way open and walked in. "What kind?"

No, no, no. Jenna didn't want to be glad to see him. She wanted to shoo him back outside. His enthusiasm and energy seemed to bounce off her living room walls like her heart banged against her ribs. He looked virile and attractive, dressed in shorts that revealed muscular legs and a No Fear T-shirt that emphasized his broad shoulders. And he wasn't, she thought with a downward glance at her damn cast, lame.

She could hate him.

"What kind of cookies?"

"I'm sure you won't like them," she told him, because most men she knew turned up their noses at anything with raisins. "Oatmeal raisin."

Much to Jenna's surprise, Stan's face lit up. "With brown sugar and cinnamon?"

"Yes, but—"

Ding. The timer went off, and Stan was practically licking his chops. "You'll need someone to test them."

"I have someone," she said. "I have me."

But Stan was already following his nose to her kitchen. "You need an objective opinion."

She hobbled after him. "From you?"

Stan grabbed the oven mitts and opened the oven door. He pulled out the cookies and made a little moaning sound. It was almost sexual, and skipped over her nerve endings in secret places. She cleared her throat.

He reverently placed the cookie sheet on the cooling rack and turned to her. "Jenna Jean, you need to understand," he began.

"Jenna," she automatically corrected. She was determined to lose her middle name.

"Jenna." He gave a low laugh. "Hell, I'll call you the Queen of England, Madam President, Your Royal Highness..."

Her lips twitched. "You must want those cookies bad."

"It's a sad, sad fact that I've eaten filet mignon, I've had champagne, I've even had chocolate mousse. But the last time I ate a hot homemade cookie was—" He broke off and shook his head. "I can't remember. It's one of the bad things about being a bachelor. C'mon Jenna J—" He swallowed the rest of her middle name with an apologetic smile and stepped closer to her. "Put me out of my misery."

Jenna took a quick breath. She wondered why his request for a cookie felt so sexual to her. Surely he didn't mean it that way. *Surely.* "You're good, Saint Stan. Let me get them off the sheet, and—"

"I'll do it," he said, and guided her to a kitchen chair. "You have a seat. You've already done the most important part."

Jenna sat there and watched Stan take the hot cookie in his hands and begin to eat it. He nibbled at the edges, slipped his tongue out to lick at a couple of crumbs, then took bites. In between bites, he made moaning noises of pleasure. The sight and sound made her warm. Lord, if he did that to a cookie, what would he do to a woman?

He snatched two more and devoured them with the same sensual attention. By the time he finished, Jenna had covered her eyes, but still peeked at him through her parted fingers.

He finally met her gaze with an expression of complete satisfaction. "Great cookies."

She nodded. "I'm glad you enjoyed them."

He brushed the crumbs off his hands. "Now it's my turn to treat you."

She hesitated as he pulled her from her seat. "That's not necessary."

"Yes, it is," he insisted. "I promised you a Sunday boat ride with your favorite drink, and I keep my promises."

"But I told you I would be busy today."

"That's okay. Your plans changed."

"No, I—"

"Jenna," he said, pulling her so close to him that she could study the cleft in his chin, his firm mouth and the generous sprinkling of spiky dark eyelashes on his eyelids. "If you don't go on this boat ride with me, I'm going to think you're scared of me."

Scared. She sucked in a sharp breath and narrowed her eyes. "That sounds like a cheap, childish dare."

"Facts is facts, m'lady."

She could smell a hint of aftershave on his jaw and

the cinnamon from the cookies on his breath. His gaze held hers with no apologies. The directness made her feel a little dizzy. He was accustomed to getting what he wanted, and Jenna was certain he didn't *really* want her.

She let out a sigh at the realization. She was going to have to *show* him that he didn't want her. "Okay," she finally said. "I'll take champagne."

"Nice boat," Jenna said, and leaned back in her chair. It was late afternoon, and many of the Sunday crowd had left. Smith Mountain Lake was quiet and beautiful.

"It's actually a yacht," Stan murmured as he cut the engine and dropped anchor. "What do you think the kids with the Youth League will think of it?"

Jenna glanced around the well-maintained deck and smiled. "Before or after they catch some flies with their open mouths?"

Stan nodded. "I guess you've answered my question. Ready for your champagne?"

"Yes," she said with a secret smile as she watched him pop the cork. He'd had to stop at three different stores to find exactly what she'd wanted. He handed a glass to her. "Thank you."

"I didn't think you'd be the champagne type," he admitted, and sat next to her with a beer.

"What type did you think I would be?"

"I don't know. White wine, maybe. Or a margarita. Why champagne?"

Because she'd wanted to annoy him? Jenna shrugged. "I like the bubbles." She looked at the tiny bubbles swimming to the top of the glass. "I always wondered what it would be like to take a bath in champagne.''

"Let me know when you decide to find out," he said in a deep voice. "I'll buy a case just to watch."

Her heart bumped, and she shook her head. She couldn't imagine Stan being content to watch. "That's okay. Sometimes wondering is more fun than doing."

"Is that a comment on some of your other experiences, too?"

He meant sex, she thought, and she had no intention of answering. "Some," she said vaguely, and looked longingly at the lake. "Right now I'm wondering how great it would feel to jump overboard. I bet the water's cooling down a little. It would feel like silk on my skin..."

She took a deep drink from her champagne and tossed Stan a wry, accusing glance. "And I would sink like a rock because of this damn cast you put on me."

He chuckled. "You'll be out of it soon. In time for the Youth League Day at the lake."

She rolled her eyes, but smiled. "Oh, you're so clever."

He shook his head. "Just an ordinary grown-up kid from Cherry Lane."

"You were never ordinary."

"No?"

"No. You could tap dance."

He shot her a dark look. "Careful," he said in a warning voice.

"If you'd have let girls up in your tree house, we wouldn't have hated you so much."

"Y'all were busy playing princess, anyway. We played pirates and airplane pilots and—"

"I sneaked up there at night sometimes."

He stopped mid-swig of his beer and stared at her. "You did?"

"Yep." She lifted her glass in a little toast. "It was great up there at night, especially when there was a breeze. The leaves whispered, and the tree would bend and sway." She smiled. "Like a ship or airplane."

"Yeah," he agreed, and his gaze grew thoughtful, gentle. She wondered at the expression.

"My dad was either totally crazy or totally great to put up that tree house."

"Maybe both? Crazy about his son and totally great."

He nodded and met her gaze, and Jenna saw a glimpse of the sadness Stan must have felt at his father's death. It made her remember what he'd been like as a boy. It made her remember they'd once been friends.

"I'm sorry he died," she said softly, and because it would have felt wrong to resist, she put her hand on his arm.

He looked down at her hand, then slowly wrapped his palm over her fingers. He looked up again to meet her gaze, and his eyes held so many emotions she couldn't read them all. But she felt them ricochet through her—loss, loneliness, love for his father.

Her heart clenched. She was pretty sure Stan didn't make a habit of exposing his vulnerabilities. He would brush them off or make a halfhearted joke. She understood because she had her own way of hiding vulnerabilities. She put up a shield of confidence, or she ran.

The seconds passed as he let her see him, and she felt the hum of a connection between them. It was a moment of wonder, of discovery, and like the kick of Scotch whiskey, it was stronger than she'd expected.

Unnerved and confused, she pulled her hand away. She heard him take a breath at the same time she did. Surely he wasn't as affected as she was.

"Thanks," he murmured.

At a loss, Jenna just nodded and took another swallow of champagne.

Stan cleared his throat. "What do you know about King Arthur's apartments?"

Jenna relaxed. "Rough place. The tenants keep the local boys in blue busy. Drugs, too much alcohol, kids without supervision. Why? You weren't planning to move there, were you?"

Stan shook his head. "No. I'm subletting near the hospital until I buy a house. There's this kid I met. He rides his bike over to the recreational blacktop for my apartments. He reminds me of Joey Caruthers."

Jenna's eyes widened in recognition. "I remember Joey. He didn't live in our neighborhood, but he played with you and the other kids a lot. One of the bad boys. Right?"

Stan nodded and rubbed his hands together. He wondered why his arm still felt warm from her touch. He wondered why his gut still felt tight from the way she'd looked at him. He rolled his shoulder. "Joey played with our group until he moved away. I never heard what happened to him, but I always got the impression he didn't have a great home life."

"And you think this boy who plays basketball at your apartment might not have a great home life, either?"

He narrowed his eyes and looked out on the water. "I can't be sure. He says his brother has custody because his parents died. This is gonna sound crazy, but Jordan, the kid, has this look in his eyes like he's a lot older on the inside than he should be."

Jenna got very quiet. "You don't think he's being abused?"

Stan thought about it and shook his head. "No."

"Neglect?"

He looked at her and assessed her. "Am I talking to the assistant commonwealth attorney or Jenna Jean Anderson?"

She hesitated, clearly struggling with the question, then she looked up at the sky. "This is a difficult area for me. I chomp at the bit to do something to help, but the system and peoples' emotions prevent it. Okay, this is Jenna Anderson, who just happens to have a little legal knowledge about these situations." She met his gaze and sort of smiled. "Will that do?"

Stan nodded, suspecting she would *do* in many ways. "I don't know about neglect, but he's in a bad environment without a lot of supervision."

"At risk."

"Yeah." She lifted her eyebrows. "There are several options. You can report the situation to child protective services. That process can be slow and painful. You can get him hooked up with the Youth League and keep an eye on him that way. There's also a Big Brother organization."

"He's got a big brother who's busy with other

things.'' He poured more champagne into her glass and stood. ''I don't know. I'll have to think about it.''

''Sounds like you're getting involved,'' she ventured. ''This kind of thing can get messy.''

''I'm learning that life can be messy,'' he told her, and moved toward her. ''You can't control all the variables.''

Her expression turned wary. ''But you can try.''

He bent down in front of her. ''It's not as much fun that way.''

''That's a matter of opinion.''

Stan watched her slip a lock of hair behind one ear. Even in her casual, white, sleeveless shirt and khaki shorts, she looked pulled together and in control on the outside. Her blue eyes, however, told a different story. She looked disrupted, perplexed and maybe just a little excited.

Stan slid his hand up to touch her silky hair. ''You're not a control freak, are you Jenna Jean?''

She shifted slightly in her seat. ''I wouldn't choose the term *freak*.''

Her tension surrounded her like a wall. But he could climb it. ''Did you ever wonder what it would be like to let go and let it rip?''

He watched her take a careful breath. ''I've wondered,'' she confessed softly, ''but I've usually thought wondering would feel better than doing.''

He moved still closer between her long legs. The one with the cast was propped to the side on a small table. ''I wonder about you,'' he said and lowered his mouth to her cheek.

''Stan,'' she said softly, the protest in her voice.

He lifted her hand to his chest. His pulse raced from being so close to her. "Can you feel my heart?"

She swallowed, excitement and confusion warring in her gaze. "Yes."

"What do you think about what you do to me? It's messy. It's out of control."

"Is it?"

He skimmed his hand down to her collarbone. "What's going on with your heart, Jenna?"

"I—"

He lowered his hand to the top of her breast, and she closed her eyes. She was so clearly torn that he felt a wave of tenderness for her. "Is it a little out of control?"

She nodded, but didn't push his hand away. He saw her nipple budding through the shirt and wondered if she had any idea how hard he was. "I want you," he told her. "I want to take off your shirt and put my mouth right here," he said, rubbing her nipple with his thumb. "Then I want to kiss you other places."

Releasing just one button, he slipped his finger to the sensitive tip of her breast. "Jenna, I wanna do more than wonder."

She bit her lip and made a soft sound of arousal and frustration. She opened her eyes and closed her hand around his wrist. "I'm all wrong for you."

Surprise darted through him. "Why?"

Her words came out in a breathless rush. "I'm— serious. Sometimes too serious. I like being in control. I'm not a good-time girl."

He frowned. "What if I don't want a good-time girl?"

She gave him a look of disbelief. "Yes, you do. You go through women like tissues."

The truth pinched, but Stan knew he had changed. "Used to," he corrected.

"I'm high maintenance."

An odd and inexplicable rush of possessiveness raced through him. He wanted her for himself. The desire went deep, the instinct strong. He leaned closer, keeping her hand against his chest so she could feel her effect on him.

"High maintenance," he said. "Maybe you're worth it."

He saw the fear and knew he'd gone too far when she said, "There's another thing. You're my doctor. You can't get involved with me. Professional integrity."

He felt the sharp truth of her words and stared at her. He couldn't think of much else she could have said that would have made him back off. He reluctantly lifted his hands away from her. The Knife had won.

Six

Jenna hadn't seen Stan in over a week, and that fact should have been okay. It should have been wonderful. It should have been terrific.

It should have been, but it wasn't.

Although she'd spent some time on the phone listening to Emily talk about how wonderful her husband Beau was, and how happy he was about the baby, Jenna had thought of Stan when she went to sleep and when she awakened. She'd thought of him during her lunch hour. To her utter dismay, she'd even thought of him in court.

If she could have successfully slapped the mold of womanizing, self-centered egomaniac on Stan, she might have been able to dismiss him. But she couldn't, because there was more than met the eye, and he'd let her see it. Worse yet, he'd let her see how she affected him.

After she'd thrown his professional integrity at him, he'd politely left her at her front door. Wrecked.

She'd forced herself to go out on two dates since then, and they'd both been disasters. One guy had bored her to tears. The other had wanted to skip dinner and find out if she was as good in the bedroom as she was in the courtroom. For once, her cast had come in handy, against Romeo's shin.

Swearing under her breath, she pushed open the door to Stan's outer office. She was here for her regular appointment, and there was *no* reason for her palms to be sweating.

After she signed in, she was ushered into Stan's office instead of an examining room. She barely had time to notice the plastic Humpty Dumpty on his desk before Stan walked through the door.

"Hi. How are you?"

Her heart picked up just from seeing him. "Fine. Is there a problem? I thought this was just a regular checkup where you assure me that my cast will come off in two weeks so I don't have to borrow my neighbor's chain saw and do it myself."

He gave a slight grin, but his eyes remained serious. "You won't need to borrow your neighbor's chain saw. There's no problem, just a change. I thought it might be best if my colleague, Dr. Abernathy, handled your case from now on."

Her breath stopped in her throat. "But—"

He held up her chart. "I've reviewed your condition with him thoroughly. He's an excellent physician. More experienced than I am, for that matter. And—"

The door whooshed open, and Dr. Abernathy, a

middle-aged man with intelligent brown eyes, walked in. "Sorry I'm late. Is this my new patient?" he asked Stan.

"Yes. Jenna Jean Anderson. Since I have a personal interest, I think it would be best if you took over." Stan gave a rough chuckle. "Just get her out of the cast and back on her feet quickly."

Dr. Abernathy turned his attention to Jenna. "Thinking of using a hacksaw on yourself?"

Dazed by the speed of the change, she gave a little nod. "Actually a chain saw."

Dr. Abernathy gave a bark of laughter. "We can't have that. Tell you what," he said. "We'll negotiate in the exam room. I'll return a quick phone call and be with you in just a minute."

She watched Stan pass the chart to him. He closed the door behind him, and complete silence filled the room. She was almost afraid to look at Stan. He'd taken a bold action, and there'd been nothing sheepish about his attitude. She admired the way he'd handled the situation; at the same time she wondered what would happen now.

"Do you think you'll be comfortable with Dr. Abernathy?" Stan asked.

She paused a half beat. His concern about her confidence was one more reason to like him. She met his gaze and saw passion and determination in his eyes. "Yes. I'm just a little surprised."

He walked around his desk and leaned against the side of it. "How long has it been since you felt like you did when we were on the yacht?"

Her stomach tightened. His gaze, his very presence

demanded the truth. "I'm not sure," she managed to say, then shook her head. "Maybe never."

He nodded. "Never. I'm scaring you spitless, aren't I?" He lifted his hand and gently smiled. "Don't answer that. I can see it on your face. Maybe this will make it easier. I'm just Stanley Michaels, after your cookies."

"Oh," Maddie said. "You're going out."

"Just for an ice cream float. No big deal," Jenna told Maddie, who had stopped by unexpectedly with her husband, Joshua, and toddler son, Davey. Truth to tell, Jenna was thankful for the distraction. She still wasn't quite sure what had possessed her to go out with Stan, even if it was for something as innocent as an old-fashioned float. "Have you talked with Emily?"

Maddie smiled. "Yep. Beau has clipped her wings. He won't let her ride the motorcycle anymore. She said he hovers worse than her mother ever did."

"And she loves it." She ruffled Davey's wild, auburn hair as he wrestled to get down from Joshua's arms.

"He's in a rush like Maddie always was," Jenna said, watching her godchild zoom toward the kitchen. Davey knew the exact location of her cookie jar.

"Yes, but I've recently learned something tragic about Davey," Maddie said in a hushed voice, her dancing eyes at odds with her serious tone. "He *loves* country music." She shuddered. "He shuns rock and roll, and it's all Joshua's fault," she said, squeezing her husband's arm and looking up at him with a playful, adoring gaze.

Joshua gave a proud grin. "The boy has excellent taste."

Jenna saw the love between Joshua and Maddie and felt a tug of longing in her heart. The sensation surprised her, and she quickly shook it off. She turned toward the kitchen. "I bet he finds those cookies in no ti—"

"Cookie!" Davey squealed.

"Bingo," Joshua echoed, and the three adults found Davey clutching a cookie in each hand, a bite out of each of them.

"Davey," Maddie said, rushing to his side. "Two is too many."

The little tike shook his head stubbornly and clutched the cookies to his chest. "My cookies."

"It's okay with me," Jenna began, "but I'm just the godmother."

Maddie held up one finger. "Please give me one cookie."

Davey frowned. "No."

Maddie sighed. "He's in that 'no' stage."

"No?" Jenna repeated.

"He says no to everything, even if he means yes."

Jenna heard the front door swing closed, then from the corner of her eye, she saw Stan walk into the room. "Ah, yes. The 'no' stage," Stan said, his gaze sliding warmly over Jenna.

Jenna felt warm all over, and *all under*. She frowned and wondered how he did that to her.

Maddie tossed a curious glance at him, then looked back at Jenna. "You oughta remember it, Jenna Jean, since you never grew out of it."

Stan gave a rough chuckle that rubbed her nerve

endings like a feather. "Nothing like an old friend to keep you grounded."

Maddie and Joshua looked at Stan. "You look familiar," she said. "Something about you—" Her eyes widened. "Omigod, it's *Stanley Michaels!*"

Jenna cringed. She had put off telling Maddie about Stan. Not that there was anything to tell, she swiftly reassured herself. She just *seemed* pleased to see him, she wasn't actually happy about it.

Stan laughed again. "Good to see you too, Maddie."

"But—"

Joshua narrowed his eyes but extended his hand. "Joshua Blackwell," he said. "You're Jenna's friend?"

"Close enough," Stan said, shaking Joshua's hand. "You must be Maddie's husband, and that little guy must be both of yours. He's got Maddie's hair and eyes and your chin. Right?"

Jenna watched Joshua take a deep breath. She could see a world of emotion in both Maddie's and Joshua's eyes. She knew that Joshua had adopted Davey, and it was clear to anyone with eyes or ears that he loved the boy like his own.

The mistake was easily made, Jenna thought, but Stan had unknowingly made a statement that affirmed Joshua. Once again, she felt a faint knocking in the region of her heart because of Stan.

"He's mine," Joshua said, and Maddie squeezed his arm before he turned to Davey. "Hey, partner, won't you share one of those with me?"

Davey, who had stuffed most of one cookie in his mouth, glanced down at the remaining cookie, then, his mouth covered with crumbs and tilted in a huge smile, he extended the cookie to Joshua to feed him.

Maddie looked at Jenna and batted her eyes. "My hero," she said in mock adoration. "He can disarm a toddler with a cookie in less than thirty seconds." Maddie, however, was distracted for only a moment. She glanced at Stan, then back to Jenna. "You're going out with Stanley Michaels."

"Stan," he corrected, and moved closer to Jenna. "Yes, she is."

"It's not really out," Jenna said, feeling his amused gaze on her.

Maddie's eyes widened. "You're staying in?"

"No!" Jenna felt Stan brush against her and swallowed. "It's just down the street," she amended in a calmer tone.

"Oh," Maddie said, her expression indicating she understood absolutely nothing and Jenna could expect an interrogation at a later date. "How did you two run into each other?"

Stan brushed against her again, glancing down at her still-gimpy leg. Jenna shifted her weight. Her leg ached. About the only two good things she could say about the leg were that it was shaven and it was castless.

"I operated on her ankle."

Maddie blinked and stood silent for a full moment. A rare event. "You're not a doctor?"

"It usually helps to be a doctor if you're going to perform surgery," Stan said, and added dryly, "especially if you're operating on a lawyer."

Maddie nodded slowly, then turned her inquisitive

gaze back to Jenna. "Jenna Jean," she said in a sing-song voice, "you've been holding out on me."

"Not really," she said. "I kept forgetting to tell you."

"Uh-huh," Maddie said in disbelief.

"I think we've finished the cookies," Joshua said, taking Davey by the hand. "Tell Jenna thank you."

Davey tugged Jenna down to give her a messy, cookie kiss. "Thanks."

Jenna's heart softened, and she kissed his forehead. "Anytime, slugger."

She glanced up to find Stan looking at her intently. Feeling the punch of his gaze as if he could see inside her, she had to take a careful breath to steady herself.

"Well, have fun on your date," Maddie said with a too-innocent smile.

"Thanks," Stan said.

"It's just ice cream," Jenna insisted, feeling her blood pressure rise. "You can't get more innocent than ice cream."

Maddie and Joshua exchanged an amused, intimate glance, then laughed lightly. "Uh-huh," Maddie said again in that disbelieving tone.

"Beware the whipped cream," Joshua murmured as he ushered Maddie and Davey past Jenna and Stan. "We'll see you soon."

After her friends left, Jenna frowned and looked at Stan. "Whipped—" She broke off when she saw the sexually knowing expression on his face.

"Cream," Stan finished. "Need a demonstration?"

"No," Jenna immediately said, a shocking image of her naked body tangled with his racing through her mind.

"Uh-huh," Stan said, mocking Maddie's tone. "Still stuck in that 'no' stage?"

Jenna resisted the urge to scream. Barely. She lifted her chin. "No."

Stan leaned closer until his face was barely an inch from hers. "Then prove it."

Jenna fought to make her lungs work. His closeness affected her knees and melted her bones. She took a careful step back. "I want my ice cream."

He matched his step to hers, eliminating the distance between them again. Jenna swallowed. He was too pushy, she told herself. That wasn't a sensual thrill making her heart race. It was annoyance.

If he kissed her, she would fix him. She wouldn't respond. It would be like kissing a dead fish. It would—

He laced his long fingers through hers, and her brain simply stopped. "Let's go," he said.

They walked the short distance to Gryder's Pharmacy, a small drugstore that still served fountain drinks, sodas, ice cream and milk shakes. Pleasantly reminiscent of a simpler time, the store catered to the settled residents of the north side of Roanoke.

"Take a seat," Stan told her. "I'll get your order."

"I'm fine," Jenna said.

"You need to resume your activities gradually. You haven't had your cast off very long."

Jenna grinned at the authoritative tone in his voice. "And you're not my doctor anymore."

He met her gaze thoughtfully, but she could practically see his mind whipping through possibilities. "How do you think those ladies at the checkout would respond if I ordered a gross of the fluorescent condoms and told the clerk to put them on your account?''

Jenna noticed the women were some very nice busybodies who lived on her street. She sat, reluctantly. ''You are evil. You love to blackmail.''

''I reserve blackmail as a last resort.'' His lips twitched, then he leaned over her. ''You just couldn't stand it when I finally beat you in one-on-one.''

She wanted to slap him. Or something. The man made her blood boil. ''I liked you better when you were short and your mother made you take tap dancing lessons. You were nicer then.''

He kissed the end of her nose, then shook his head. ''Chocolate or vanilla float, Jenna? We're here to celebrate your freedom.''

Surprised at the brief affectionate gesture, she blinked. ''Chocolate,'' she managed to say, and watched him walk toward the counter.

He kept her off guard. One moment he was all gentlemanly consideration and charm. The next, he was invading her space. If she were honest, she couldn't say which she liked better.

He returned with the floats. Jenna took a sip and sighed. ''It's wonderful. Thanks.''

''My pleasure.'' He glanced down at her leg. ''Feel a few pounds lighter?''

''Yes.'' She twirled the float with her straw. ''I've been thinking about the Youth League Day at the lake. Since there's going to be waterskiing—''

''Not for you. If you strain it, your recovery will take that much longer.''

''I could slalom.'' She gave a slight grin. ''Look, Ma, one ski.''

He shook his head. "Absolutely not." She was the most indomitable woman he'd ever met, and part of him thought he was damn crazy for getting involved with her. But it seemed the most natural course in the world for him to get close to her. She drew him like a beacon in the night, and he was compelled to learn her inside and out.

Every once in a while, he felt a sliver of unease that he might not be able to control the direction of the relationship the way he had in the past with other women. Silly, he thought. He'd had a good time, but he'd always kept his balance with women. There was no reason he shouldn't be able to keep his balance with Jenna.

He felt her blue gaze on him.

"What are you thinking?" she asked.

"That you are the most stubborn and persistent woman I've met."

She looked down her nose at him. "I told you before that I prefer the term *determined.*"

"And Princess Jenna gets what Princess Jenna wants. Right?"

"Not princess," she corrected. Her lips twitched, and she looked as if she couldn't decide whether to tell or not.

Curious, Stan grinned. "Not princess. Then what?"

Her gaze was reluctant.

"C'mon," he coaxed. "If not princess?"

"Queen," she said, the determination in her eyes sexy enough to melt the ice cream in both their floats. "I want to rule."

He quickly swallowed his mouthful before he laughed. How, he wondered, did she amuse him at the same time she aroused him? "And how do you plan to *rule?*"

Her smile of triumph faded. "Well, I was going to be a judge, but that may not happen until my next life. That's another story."

He lifted his hand. "Hey, wait a minute. Why another lifetime?"

She shrugged. "Politics, white hat-itis. It doesn't matter," she said, but he suspected it did. The wounded expression was fleeting, and she covered it quickly, but it grabbed at him. Another color of Jenna, and he wanted to see them all.

"You did something nice without knowing it," she continued, changing the subject, "when you told Joshua and Maddie you could tell Davey belonged to them. Joshua adopted him after he and Maddie got married." She smiled. "He's incredibly possessive of both of them, so you probably made his day."

"I wouldn't have guessed he was adopted," Stan said, "by either of them."

"Joshua's crazy about Maddie and Davey. A lot of love there," Jenna said, her eyes softening.

If Stan didn't know better, he might have detected a hint of longing. "Did you ever have anyone feel that way about you?"

Her eyes widened and she hesitated. "Not that I know of." She met his gaze. "What about you?"

"I have generally tried not to encourage it." This was one of the areas he was dissatisfied about in his life, and he was rethinking. "Too close for comfort before. And you?"

She nodded. "That and giving up the control. If you love that much, then losing would be unbearable.'' Her eyes narrowed in a slight flinch. ''The hurt would be terrible.''

''Your float's melting,'' he reminded her, lifting the straw to her lips. He felt that same tug, a gentle urgency to get closer. It confused the hell out of him. ''Maybe it's about taking risks. Finding someone worth the risk.''

Her gaze met his, and he saw the connecting emotions mirrored on her face. He also saw the confusion. ''Maybe,'' she said in a quiet voice, and he could tell she was looking at him differently.

After they finished the floats, they strolled back to Jenna's street. It was a warm, dark night, and he noticed she started to favor her right leg as they approached the hill.

Stan stopped and guided her off the road. ''Time for a change in transportation,'' he said.

She looked at him blankly. ''Pardon?''

''I'm giving you a ride fit for a queen.'' He pointed to his back. ''Piggyback.''

Jenna immediately shook her head. ''Oh, no. That's not necessary.''

''You'd rather limp?'' Stan asked, then lifted his hand. ''Don't answer that. Okay. It's either piggyback or get thrown over my shoulder. Your choice.''

She lifted her chin. ''It's really not necessary.''

''Yes, it is.''

''You're getting pushy again.''

''And you're being stubborn.''

They stood there glaring at each other, neither willing to budge an inch. ''You know how you hated it when I got big enough to beat you in one-on-one?''

''Yes,'' she said in a dark voice.

"Well, think of this as the benefit. I'm big enough to carry you, too."

"You're a bully. I don't want you to carry me," she told him, and began to limp away.

If there hadn't been a hint of humor in her accusation, he might have felt stung. Instead, he made a tsking sound and went after her. "There you go, making those generalizations again."

Hooking his arm around her waist, he drew her against him and felt her stiffen immediately. He lowered his voice and spoke softly in her ear. "I like you. I don't want your ankle to hurt."

She sighed and her body softened. "You make it hard for me not to like you when you're kind," she confessed in an equally low voice.

Stan slowly turned her around to face him. "Is that so?"

"Yes, it is. So you need to stop."

Her eyes were dark and moody, wanting and resisting. Her hair looked like black silk reflecting the moonlight. Her voice was like a hand on his thigh, stroking close to the heat of him, teasing, but not quite satisfying. He suspected, however, that this woman could satisfy him in ways he'd never been satisfied.

He leaned closer to smell her clean, feminine scent.

"You're not going to kiss me, are you?"

He wanted to. Wanted to do more than kiss her. He wanted to taste her lips and slip his hands beneath her shirt and feel her soft skin, the pucker of her nipple against his palm, then in his mouth. He wanted to slide his hand between her thighs and make her moist and ready for him. He wanted...too much at the moment.

Sucking in a mind-clearing breath, he shook his head. "Nope, you're going to kiss me." He bent slightly and glanced over his shoulder. "Hop on."

"Why am I going to kiss you?" she asked.

"Because you're going to be so grateful that you didn't have to drag your aching leg up that hill. Hop on."

She frowned, but got on his back and curled her hands around his shoulders. He supported her legs with his hands and walked up the hill. "I haven't been carried piggyback in a long time," she muttered.

The gentle pressure of her breasts on his back tried his patience. When he reached her driveway, he started to run.

Jenna shrieked and held tight. "What are you doing?"

"I wouldn't want to be accused of not giving you a good ride." He stopped when he reached the porch. When she slid down, he turned to face her.

She looked uneasy. "Are you sure you wouldn't rather have a cookie?"

Stan bit back a smile. "I'm sure."

"What if I don't want to kiss you?"

Stan called her bluff. "Are you saying you don't? Is that the truth?"

Her gaze fell from his and she sighed. "I don't have a thirty second rule," she warned.

"That's fine," he said. "You lead."

She lifted her gaze to him again. He looked into her eyes and wondered at all her uncertainty. He saw want and reluctance. The power of the wanting was gratifying. The reluctance affected his heart. "I must be insane,'' she whispered, clearly fighting the sexual energy flaring between them.

Her gaze locked with his, she leaned closer and closer until he lost focus and her lips touched his.

He didn't try to withhold a groan when her breasts pressed against his chest. The sound seemed to encourage her. She opened her mouth and slid her tongue past his lips. He could feel the passion stirring to life inside her. Her breath was short, her body restless.

Stan felt a shot of pure sexual adrenaline, and he began to eat her mouth. He felt her arms climb up his shoulders, plastering the length of her lean, sexy body against his, and he bracketed his hands around her hips, drawing her into his hardness.

Arousal pulsed through him. It wasn't soft. It wasn't easy. It wasn't controlled. ''Oh, Jenna,'' he muttered against her mouth as he rocked against her. He wanted to be driving into her softness.

''It's not enough,'' he said, sliding his hands into the back of her shorts to her bare bottom and guiding her to make the ache better, and worse.

She undulated in a sinuous, rocking rhythm that made him groan. ''Let's go inside,'' he said.

She made a sound of frustration and pulled back. Her eyes nearly black with arousal, she stared at him in confusion. ''This is all wrong,'' she whispered. ''I'm all wrong for you.''

Stan's body protested Jenna's absence. ''What in hell are you talking about?''

He saw the disconcerting expression flash across her face when she glanced at her trembling hands. She looked away from him and shook her head. ''I'm all wrong for you. You date agreeable women with names like Cookie or Cherry or—'' she rolled her shoulder in frustration ''—other food names. You date women who probably tell you how wonderful you are. They're free and breezy and don't take life too seriously. They probably fit into every social situation imaginable.''

Stan narrowed his eyes. ''I've dated some women like that. So what?''

She took a careful breath. ''So I'm not like that. I've tried to explain this to you before. I'm not free and breezy. I'm too serious. Besides, I'm not all that—'' she hesitated ''—experienced.''

Stan mentally flipped through the possibilities. She couldn't mean— ''You're talking about sexual experience.''

She bit her lip. He hadn't seen her do that since she was a kid.

''Yes, so I'm probably not as creative or exciting or—''

Stan gave a rough chuckle. ''Now, who's joking?''

Her gaze met his, and Stan realized he'd made a huge miscalculation. Somewhere, somehow, Jenna Jean had gotten a skewed view of her sexual appeal. ''I think we need to review,'' he said. ''Give me your hand.''

''This isn't neces—''

''I know. Just humor me,'' he told her, and pressed her hand against his chest. ''Feel my heart. Still racing from holding you. I'm still hot.'' He took a breath at the feminine curiosity in her eyes. ''Still hard.'' He stepped closer and pulled her against him. ''I want you to touch me,'' he whispered. ''I want to touch you. I want to know you, all of you. It may not make sense, but I can tell you know it, too."

He could feel the struggle in her tense body. "I don't know what to do with you."

He gave another rough chuckle. "I can offer some suggestions."

"This is so easy for you. You've got the right words, the smooth moves. But it's more than smooth moves for me. Being intimate means more." She gave a shaky sigh and pulled back from him. "Right now I think I'd better say thank you for the float." Her eyes wide and vulnerable, she reached for the door. "Good night."

Struggling with a new, overwhelming sense of emptiness, he nodded. "G'night, Queen Jenna Jean."

She managed a half smile. "Just Jenna, Stanley."

He waited until she closed the door. The energy they'd generated from talking and touching still echoed around him, sinking into his bloodstream. He could feel it thrumming inside him, exhilarating, frustrating.

He looked at the door and imagined her walking in her house, trying to shake free of the overwhelming sensations, trying to regain control, searching for her peace of mind. She was like him in that respect.

He shook his head and smiled grimly. "You can run, sweetheart, but you can't hide."

Seven

Forty-two kids descended on Smith Mountain Lake the second weekend in July. Mitzi, the current Youth League chairman, had done her job well. One adult for every two kids, plus lifeguards. Jenna had been told her role was to direct traffic and help supervise the morning swim clinic. Since several of the kids hadn't learned how to swim, the Youth League provided a couple hours of lessons combining fun and safety.

She hadn't seen Stan yet. She wouldn't look for him, she told herself. It appalled her that she hadn't gotten herself under control about him until the past two days. Hot flashes. Illicit thoughts. Fantasies. Dreams. Ridiculous.

"Hi, beautiful."

Jenna heard the words, but dismissed them as she

adjusted her sunglasses on top of her head. No one had ever called her beautiful.

She felt a tug on her hair and swiveled her head to see Stan.

"I'm talking to you, Queen Jenna," he said in a low voice.

He was dressed in swim trunks and a tank top that showed off his athletic form, broad shoulders, well-developed chest and biceps, flat stomach and hard thighs. *And he felt as good as he looked.* Jenna bit back an oath and swallowed. "I'm not beautiful. And I'm not queen, yet," she told him.

His gaze fell over her like warm honey. "That's a matter of perspective. Your leg's looking good. If you try to take a lot of little breaks, you'll last longer," he said, and before she could open her mouth, continued. "But since you like to argue, you'll probably ignore my wisdom and be hurting by mid-afternoon." He brushed a strand of her hair from her face. "If that happens, just come to me and I'll find a place for you in the shade with a drink."

Feeling like she was going up the down elevator, Jenna stared at him. How did he do that? One moment he was giving orders, the next he was taking the sting out of them by saying something nice. Her heart hammered against her rib cage. She could get to like this, she thought, but for the sake of her mental health, she'd better not.

She swallowed. "I told you to stop being nice."

His lips tilted in a slow, sexy grin that did crazy things to her insides. "One of your rules?"

"Yes."

"Some rules are meant to be broken." He glanced

around at the crowd of kids headed for the water. "I'm in charge of the boat activities this afternoon. What are you doing?"

"Directing," Jenna said. "Mitzi also told me if anyone gets out of line she wants me to inform them I make my living prosecuting criminals."

"So you're the muscle today?"

She slid a sideways glance at him. "In a manner of speaking. I hope it's just a safe, fun day."

"Yeah." He nodded at a boy walking toward him. "Here's someone I want you to meet. Jenna Anderson, this is Jordan Goff."

The name rang a bell. His eyes held a world-weary look, and something about the lanky boy seemed vaguely familiar. She extended her hand. "Nice to meet you, Jordan."

"You, too," Jordan said awkwardly.

Jenna narrowed her eyes. "Do you have an older brother?" She searched her memory. "His name is— it starts with a *T*."

"Tim," Jordan said, his eyes growing wary. "Yeah, he's my brother."

Jenna nodded, but said nothing else about Jordan's brother. She suspected Tim might be a sore subject, since he'd been charged with several misdemeanors. "Have you ever been on water skis before?"

Still clearly on guard, Jordan shrugged. "Nope, but Dr. Stan says I'll probably be doing slalom by the end of the day."

"That's more than I'll be doing," Jenna muttered.

"You can't water-ski?" Jordan asked.

"I've been told my ankle's not ready," Jenna said,

shooting a dark look at Stan. "I broke it playing basketball."

Jordan's eyes widened, and she could see his estimation of her rose dramatically. "She plays?" he said to Stan.

Stan nodded. "She used to beat me in one-on-one."

Jenna smiled. "Until he grew."

"Cool." Jordan looked from Jenna to Stan. "I beat him now."

Stan gave a mock scowl. "Stop bragging and get in the water."

Jordan took off for the lake, and Jenna felt Stan's gaze on her. "What do you know about Tim?"

She shook her head. "It's not great, could be worse. Everything after age eighteen is a matter of public record."

Stan grimaced. "I wonder how hard it would be for me to adopt Jordan."

Jenna gaped at him. "You're kidding. This is more than taking on a puppy. Even though he's thirteen, if you take on the responsibility of a child, he's yours more than legally. He's yours emotionally. And believe me, they are not always gone by age eighteen. It's much more than a five-year commitment."

Stan's jaw tightened. "Are you suggesting," he asked in a deliberately mild tone, "that I don't have the staying power to be a parent?"

Jenna felt a sinking sensation in her stomach. She'd spoken impulsively, and she shouldn't have. Worse yet, she had her suspicions about why she kept trying to paint Stan black, and that knowledge brought her no comfort. "No, I just—"

He stopped her dead with his gaze. "You underestimate me, Jenna."

Her throat tightened, but surprisingly, the words came with ease. "I'm sorry."

He lifted his eyebrows in surprise. "An apology?"

"Yes. I was wrong. I shouldn't have jumped down your throat with both feet like that."

He shook his head, studying her intently and leaning closer to her. "Are you concerned with being fair or with my opinion?"

She felt caught, didn't want to confess, but his gaze demanded the truth. Jenna held her breath. With Stan, she always felt as if she were trying to turn cartwheels on the balance beam. Jenna had never been very good on the balance beam. She swallowed and said, "Both."

He sifted his fingers through her hair, and his expression gentled. "My opinion is you're the fairest woman I know."

She liked his hands in her hair. She liked the tone of his voice. Intimate, honest. "Thank you."

"My opinion is that you're also a chicken."

Jenna blinked. She stared at him and drew back. "Pardon?"

"You're a chicken," Stan said in an unbelievably sexy voice. He made a low clucking sound and his lips twitched in a grin. "You want to be with me, but you're afraid."

Resisting the urge to say "Am not!," she sucked in a quick breath of indignation. "You are the most conceited man in the universe."

"Scaredy-cat," he returned in a mild tone.

Her temper spiked. "I wish I was still wearing that damn cast, so I could kick you with it."

"The truth cuts like a knife, doesn't it?"

That stopped her. If she'd been chewing bubble-gum, he might as well have smacked a bubble right on her face. There was no malice in his tone, however. Gentle, come-play-with-me humor. There was a glint of the old Stanley who'd been her pal before they'd hit puberty. No defenses left for her but the truth.

It wasn't the easiest thing to do, but she held his gaze for a moment. "Yeah, I'm scared. So what are you gonna do about it?"

Jenna continued to direct traffic until lunch, when the kids gathered around grills and tables loaded with hot dogs, hamburgers, chips and sodas. Sitting on a stretch of grass under a tree, she was just finishing her burger when Stan and Jordan showed up.

"Share the shade? I brought you a cookie," Stan said, then sat beside her before she could answer. "You're dry. You're supposed to be wet."

"I'm not getting wet," Jenna said, wondering why he looked so good even with his hair wet from a swim. "If I can't ski, I'm not going in at all."

Stan chuckled. "Are we pouting?"

"No," she said, but laughed because he was right. She loved the water.

"I can help."

"Not neces—"

"Necessary. Oh, but it is."

Wary of the wicked expression on his face, Jenna shook her head. "You—"

The distinctive, loud buzz of a motorcycle roared through the air, catching her attention.

Stan and Jordan glanced at the oncoming Harley with interest. "Is this one of the Youth League kids who's running late?"

The motorcycle rider cut his engine and dismounted. "No," Jenna said, then identified the rider when he pulled off his helmet. She smiled. "I should have known it was Ben."

"Ben... Hey it's Ben Palmer! Maddie's brother," Stan said as he stood. "Haven't seen him in years."

Jenna winced as Ben let out a wild call and headed toward them. "Oh, no." She looked at Jordan. "Don't watch this. It's disgusting."

Jordan's lips lifted in a semismile.

"Stan-My-Man!" Ben called, and gave Stan a bear hug. "Maddie told me you're back in town and you're a doctor, for Pete's sake."

"Bad-Ben," Stan returned, shaking his head in amazement. "You look like you've taken over the local Hog club."

Jenna watched the two of them laugh at each other. They performed some sort of convoluted handshake. Then they spit in the grass. "Bad Boys forever," Ben said.

Jordan looked at Jenna, his face full of questions. "What are they doing?"

"They used to be in a club together. You just witnessed their disgusting secret handshake. Do everyone a favor and please forget you ever saw it."

Ben glanced down at her and grinned. "Jenna Jean, how ya' doing? I heard about your leg." He tossed her a playfully suggestive look. "Looks pretty good to me. Maddie told me Stan took care of you."

She just laughed and stood. "My leg's fine. Stan took care of it at the hospital." She quickly switched the subject before Ben could start razzing her about Stan. "Where are you working this week? Last I heard, you were a bouncer."

"I'm a mechanic at the foreign car shop. I worked this morning. That's why I just got here."

"So you're staying out of trouble?"

He plastered an innocent expression on his face. "I always stay out of trouble." He glanced at Jordan. "Right?"

Jordan, who didn't know Ben from a tree trunk, but clearly identified with anyone who drove a motorcycle, nodded. "Right."

Stan glanced curiously from Jenna to Ben. "It sounds like you two have kept in touch."

"Oh, yeah," Ben said, and wrapped his arm around Jenna's waist. "Jenna and I have something in common."

Stan raised his eyebrows. "Is that so?"

"Yep." Ben nodded. "Something that will bind us together for life."

The barest hint of confusion, then something darker, glinted in Stan's eyes. "What's that?" he asked in a cool voice.

Jenna rammed her elbow in Ben's ribs. "We're godparents to Maddie's son. I pray every night that Maddie will live to be a hundred, not because I don't adore Davey. I would take him in a minute. I just don't think I could face the arguments Ben and I would have about Davey's future."

"You'd make him a sissy," Ben told her.

"You'd make him a hoodlum," Jenna returned.

Stan stepped between them. "Peace."

"She knows I'm a great guy," Ben said to Stan. "Listen, let me grab a burger, and I'll talk to you later, *Doc*."

Stan nodded. "Great seeing you."

Turning to Jenna after Ben left and Jordan went off to join the other kids, Stan ran his finger down the inside of her arm. "So you know he's a great guy, huh?"

The nerve endings in her arm buzzed. Uncertain of Stan's tone, she shrugged and sat down. "Beneath the leather and tattoo, he's a nice guy. There was a time I was afraid he might be working in a chop shop for stolen automobile parts, but he wasn't. He's just still going through his rebel phase." She tossed a meaningful glance at Stan. "Some men *never* grow out of it."

"Good thing," he said as he sat down again. "Haven't you heard? Rebels make great lovers."

Jenna choked on her soft drink. "Brief lovers," she finally managed to say. "Here today, gone tomorrow."

He leaned closer to her. "There's only one way to find out," he said next to her ear, then gazed at her with an enigmatic expression on his face. "Am I making you nervous?"

Although her instinct was to deny, deny, deny, she said, "Yes".

His brown eyes made satin sheet promises. "I can help." His voice was butter soft with invitation. He lifted his cookie. "Want a bite?"

* * *

Later that afternoon Jenna overheard a couple of the adult volunteers when she sat behind a tree to rest her ankle.

"Have you seen the guy with the boat?" one woman with a high-pitched voice asked.

"Yacht," the other woman corrected.

"He's gorgeous and single."

"And an orthopedic doctor with a reputation for being a lady-killer."

"A body *and* a brain. Ooh, he can jump my bones anytime," the one with the high voice said.

"You want me to introduce you?" the other asked as they walked away.

Jenna frowned. The women's assessment of Stan banged around in her head. She felt as if she were on a precipice with him. Balancing this way and that so she wouldn't fall. In the meantime, someone else could easily catch Stan's attention. It wouldn't matter to her, she told herself. It *shouldn't* matter to her. Throughout the rest of the afternoon, she told herself it didn't matter, but Jenna felt something green ooze through her veins.

It was almost time to leave when Jordan told her Stan needed some extra Band-Aids. Jenna collected them and took them onto the yacht at the end of the dock.

"Jenna," Stan said as she approached him. "Do you agree that these kids need an outlet for their excess energy and frustration?"

She looked at him warily, but nodded. "Yes, that's why we have Youth League."

"But, Jenna, sometimes playing basketball and waterskiing and swimming just aren't enough."

His expression of mock concern furthered her suspicions, but the large group of kids on the boat crowding around her trapped her from leaving. "I hesitate to ask," she said, "but what *would* be enough?"

He wrapped his arm around her. "I think they need to release their frustrations in a psychological way."

Jenna heard a snicker from one of the kids. "Such as?"

He tightened his arm and picked her up. "Throwing the commonwealth attorney into the lake."

The kids roared with applause.

She licked her lips. She was more afraid of the gleam in Stan's eye than the water. "I'm not the commonwealth attorney."

"You're the assistant commonwealth attorney." Stan grinned. "Close enough," he said, and tossed her overboard.

Stan had jumped in after Jenna, and although she assured him she didn't need his help, he hauled her out of the lake. Learning that his assistance had infuriated her more than his throwing her into the lake, he had to do a lot of fast talking to get her to ride home with him.

Even so, the car was a little steamy during the drive. He dropped off Jordan at the empty apartment. It appeared his neighbors were gearing up for a Saturday-night party.

Stan swore under his breath as he drove away. "I hate leaving him there."

"I'm sure you hate it, but there's not much else you can do."

"Not now," he said. "He has my phone number and beeper number. I think he'll call if it gets too crazy."

"Jordan's lucky," Jenna said. "There are a lot of kids in situations like his who have no one to call. He's very lucky."

Stan shrugged, but her words slid inside him like a warm blanket. "It seemed like the natural thing to do. It hasn't been a problem." He glanced at her. "Unlike you."

He felt her gaze on him. "Unlike *me?*"

"Yeah." He headed for her subdivision. "It's easy to see that it would be natural for you and me to be together. But you're making problems."

"*Me,*" she repeated again. "I'm not the one pushing you to do anything. I'm not the one throwing you overboard from a yacht just to give the Youth League a good laugh."

Stan shook his head. "It was for more than laughs. I told you it was to help release their frustration."

Jenna snorted in disbelief. "Then why didn't you let them toss *you* overboard?"

"Easy. You represent more of an authority figure. Plus," he added before she could take another turn with the argument, "I was already wet. And you *wanted* to go in the lake. You were just pouting because Dr. Abernathy wouldn't let you water-ski. Throwing you in the lake was for your own good."

Jenna made a sound of amazement. "And I suppose you think I should *thank* you for throwing me in?"

Stan smothered a grin as he turned onto her street. He liked that idea. "Yes. You should. You can thank me after I help you out of your wet clothes."

"How long has it been since your most recent psychological analysis, Stan? I think you may be overdue."

Stan chuckled and took her hand in his. "Jenna, you can't be too mad at me for throwing you overboard or you wouldn't have ridden home with me."

"I can take a joke," she said, sticking to her view.

"As long as it's under control," he added, wondering if she realized how her fingers curled around his.

"I didn't get upset with you until you wanted to *help* me afterward."

Pulling into her driveway, he nodded. "Independence, control."

"And the only reason I rode home with you was it gave me the opportunity to get your seat wet with the drenched clothes I'm wearing."

He cut the engine, set the emergency break and tugged her closer until her face was inches from his. "Now that's where you're wrong," he told her in a low voice.

He watched her take a quick little breath. "How?"

He rubbed his finger over the silky skin of her chin. "Because you have rules about taking rides, and I bet you don't ride with someone unless you want to."

Her eyes were watchful and full of secret seduction. He waited for her to respond, but she didn't say a word. The silence between them thickened. He skimmed his finger over her lips and watched her eyes darken still more. "You rode home with me," he whispered, "because you like being with me."

Her eyelids fluttered, but the arousal he'd glimpsed in her gaze made his heart pump harder. Moving his lips to her ear, he nuzzled her. "Jenna Jean, when are you going to let me in?"

She gave a soft sigh. "I can't invite you in my house tonight. It's a wreck. I'm a wreck. I—"

He stopped her words with a kiss, although this time his thirty second rule cost him. She tasted sweet and warm, and her tongue tangled with his as if she were as hungry for him as he was for her. By the time he pulled back, he was hard and groaning.

"You misunderstand," he said, surprised at the huskiness in his voice. "I'm not talking about your house." He put his finger against her forehead. "I want inside here," he told her. Then he lowered his hand to where her heart beat as fast as his. "And here. I want inside you, Jenna, in every possible way."

She closed her eyes. "Oh, Stan, you—you—" She swallowed. "You're too close. I can't think."

He pulled back half an inch. "How's this?"

Jenna sighed and opened her eyes. She looked overwhelmed, as if she were sinking and couldn't swim. "Try one hundred paces." She licked her lips. "Or the next block…or the next county."

He chuckled and shook his head, drawing her into his arms again. "You just need to get used to me," he told her. "You need to spend more time with me. Tonight would be a good start."

"Tonight?" she asked, confusion filtering through her voice.

"Yes. All night." He rubbed his lips over her forehead.

"No. Not all night."

"Not all night."

"Not tonight," Jenna said, lifting her head to meet his gaze.

His gut tightened. He heard the possibility in her words, saw the maybe in her eyes. She wasn't sure yet, he thought, but she would be. "Can I see you tomorrow?"

She nodded. "Yes—" She stopped, then winced and shook her head. "No. I can't. I—oh this is crazy."

He dipped his head to catch her gaze again. "What? What's crazy?"

She blew her bangs off her forehead. "I can't because I have a date."

Speechless, he felt his stomach sink to his feet. An extraordinary sensation. It took a moment before pride kicked in. "A *date?*"

She wouldn't look at him. "Yes. It's a corporate attorney I met at a luncheon last week. He asked me out, and I have made this, well, resolution to try to go out more and—"

"Then go out with me."

She hesitated. "I did that. I thought if I went out with someone else it would help."

His blood pressure climbed up the scale. *"Help?"*

She bit her lip. "Yes. I thought seeing someone else might, uh, give me some balance, help my perspective, keep me from—" She broke off and finally looked at him. "Keep me from doing something very foolish like falling for you."

If she didn't look so vulnerable, so emotionally bare and honest, he would have punched out the window. He rubbed his hand over his face. "Let me get this straight. You think going out with this guy is going to protect you from what you could feel for me."

"I was hoping."

He shook his head. "It's not going to happen, Jenna. He'll bore you to tears and you'll find your attention wandering. He'll touch you and you'll feel annoyed. The evening will drag. And if he kisses you," he told her, feeling his blood pressure rise again, "you'll wish it was me."

His name was Ned. He was well mannered, attractive and intelligent, and he clearly appreciated Jenna's intelligence. He took her to dinner at The Library, one of Roanoke's finest and most romantic restaurants.

Determined not to think of Stan, she focused on her conversation with Ned. When her attention began to slip, she found herself staring into the candlelight, seeing Stan's face.

Ned touched her hand and smiled, and Jenna waited, prayed, for a flicker of interest inside her. Nothing. Her stomach sank. He was fairly agreeable, probably controllable. Despite her best efforts, she kept imagining what Stan would have said, and how he would have joked with the waiter. He would have flirted with her outrageously and never let her forget he wanted her sexually, and that she wanted him sexually.

Stop!

She tried hard, so hard that she barely noticed the

food. Each minute felt like three. By the end of the meal, she felt exhausted. Jenna mentally waved a flag of surrender and pleaded a headache. She felt guilty when Ned, all concern and consideration, took her home and promised to call. Drawing a deep breath of relief that he didn't try to kiss her, she swept inside her home and sank glumly onto her sofa.

Sitting in the dark, Jenna folded and unfolded her hands. She felt trapped and miserable, close to tears. She wanted Stan desperately, but she was afraid to want him. The power of her feelings for him shook her.

The strength was shocking, overwhelming. She felt both dread and certainty that even though she usually exercised a great deal of mental control over her life, she couldn't deny her heart any longer.

Sighing, she hid her face in her hands. A thousand what-ifs ran through her mind. She couldn't. She shouldn't.

But she did.

He had given her his telephone number and told her to call anytime. She wished he would call now, but her phone remained silent. Moments ticked by, and Jenna grew too restless to bear it.

Needing to hear his voice, she ran to the kitchen and picked up the phone. With trembling hands, she dialed his number. She almost hung up at the sound of the first ring, but something inside her wouldn't allow her.

"Hello."

His voice reached inside her like a gentle, intimate stroke. Her heart hammering against her rib cage, she took a careful breath.

"Hello," he repeated.

Jenna swallowed over the lump in her throat. "Stan," she managed.

"Jenna? What—"

"You were right, damn you. You were right. Why aren't you here?" she asked, and closed her eyes at the need in her voice.

Eight

I'm on my way.

Stan's words vibrated inside Jenna. Moments later she was still sitting in the same chair, staring at the phone. She hadn't made a sound, but her self-defenses were screaming bloody murder.

In a matter of minutes Stan would be pounding on her door.

A sliver of panic raced through her. She should call him back. She should tell him she was okay. She would see him tomorrow when she'd regained her sanity. And if she hadn't regained it tomorrow, she'd see him Tuesday.

She picked up the phone to call, and her doorbell sounded. Her heart leapt. *Too late.* Now she needed a plan, and there was no time for one.

Taking a deep breath, she walked slowly toward

the front of her house, hoping for inspiration, but none came. She opened the door, and he immediately swept into her foyer, crowding the small area with the force of his sensual energy.

His eyes were hot and searching as he moved closer to her. "I wondered how much longer it would take," he told her.

"Take for what?"

"For you to realize you belong to me."

Her heart slammed against her rib cage. Some small, squeaky part of her logical, liberated mind protested his ownership, but at that moment, her body and heart ruled.

He lowered his mouth to hers in a mind-robbing, thigh-melting open-mouth kiss that promised, seduced and claimed. His body was flush against hers, leaving her with no mistake about his arousal. Rocking his pelvis between her thighs, he made her buzz with need. Panic ceded to passion, and Jenna began to tremble.

Stan groaned. "Why do I feel like I've wanted you since I was born?"

He kissed her as if he wanted to consume her, sliding one of his hands down her hip possessively. He swore. "I want you now."

Jenna clung to his shoulders and distantly felt something bump against her arm. Caught in the fever pitch of his mouth and hands, she could barely breathe. She felt the object bump against her arm again and frowned. "What—"

He wouldn't allow her to drag her lips from his. His tongue teased and taunted hers, provoking her response.

"What," she tried again, jerking her head to the side and gulping in air. She glanced down and saw a rectangular box. "What do you have in your hand?"

Stan squeezed her hip and darted his tongue out to taste her neck. "I'm holding you," he muttered, then groaned.

She bit back her own moan. "No. I—mean—" When he slipped his knee between her legs, though, she couldn't stop her little sound of need. "In your other hand."

He continued to rub his mouth over her neck, suckling the sensitive skin. Jenna shuddered.

"Other hand," he repeated, and sighed. Clearly reluctant, he drew his mouth away and looked at his other hand. Brief silence followed, then he gave a rough chuckle.

Confused, she stared at him, still holding on to him for support.

He quickly bussed her lips with his. "Who did you go out with tonight?"

"Why?"

He chuckled again. "Don't cross-examine right now, Counselor. Just answer the question."

Uncertain of his sanity, she shook her head. "Ned Thompson."

He nodded. "Well, I brought a little present for good ol' Ned." His lips tilted upward in a cocky grin, but his eyes were serious. "Next time you see him, give him these tissues. He's gonna need them because he'll be crying when you tell him you're not going out with him anymore."

Stunned at his possessiveness, Jenna blinked. "If I

weren't in this position, I might find that a little presumptuous."

"You mean if you weren't wrapped around me like a honeysuckle vine, and if I wasn't wanting to take you against this wall," he said, tossing the box of tissues to the floor and sliding his hands under her skirt. He lifted it inch by breathtaking inch over her hips.

Jenna's heart raced into overdrive. "We aren't *really* going to—" she swallowed "—do this here, are we?"

"Sweetheart," he told her as he slipped his fingers inside her panties, "we can do this anywhere you want."

He caressed her intimately and took her mouth again, his tongue gently thrusting in a rhythm that turned her to liquid.

"You're so wet," he said with rough approval as he slid his finger inside her. "So sweet."

She felt swollen and needy, hot and desperate for more. He was close, but she wanted him closer.

He rubbed his open mouth against hers and unzipped her dress. "I want you every way at once," he muttered. "Every way a man can have a woman."

Gently nudging her against the wall, he pulled the dress down her arms and kissed her skin as he bared it. He tugged her bra strap down with his teeth, skimmed his lips over the top of her breast, then took her aching nipple into his mouth.

Jenna felt herself clench around his finger and moaned. Eager to feel his bare skin against hers, she tugged loose the buttons of his shirt.

He continued to suckle the tip of her breast and

fondle her with his fingers. She tightened like a coil from the inside out. "Stan, please," she whispered.

"What do you want, babe?" he asked, skimming his lips over her rib cage and belly. He sent her dress sliding down to the floor in a pool of black at her feet. "What do you want?"

His voice was too sexy, and she was too susceptible.

She couldn't name what she wanted except him. When he moved his mouth lower and pressed his lips against the triangle of silk covering her femininity, she gasped. The sensation was warm and wicked, too pleasurable to bear.

"Oh, my—"

"Too much?" he murmured.

Thankful for the support of the wall and Stan's strong hands bracing her hips, Jenna moved her head in a circle. She wanted their clothes to evaporate. She wanted nothing between them, not even air. She wanted his skin on hers, she wanted him inside her. "Stan," she said, "I—"

"Not too much," he muttered. "Better hold on, Jenna. I want more of you." He stripped her panties down her legs and took her with his mouth. The sensual stroke of his tongue on her most sensitive, secret place made her shudder all over. Breathless, she felt like a bow stretched too taut. He consumed her as if he couldn't get enough of her, as if he might never get enough of her.

The thought was too much for her. It touched the core of her, the very heart of a secret wish she hadn't even realized she'd had. Her pleasure spiked, sending her up and over. A sob broke from her throat, and she shattered. She urged him upward. Shocking, unbidden tears coursed down her cheeks. "I need you," she said in a husky, desperate voice she'd never heard before. "I need you."

"Jen," he said, arousal and surprise swelling in his tone.

With shaking hands, she fumbled with his belt and button. "Help," she whispered.

Help, he did, shoving his jeans and briefs down. As soon as he was bare to her, she took his hardened masculinity in her hands and stroked. He swore. "Give me a minute."

"Too long," she said, rubbing her thumb over the already moist tip of him.

Stan swore again and moved her hand away.

Distraught, she met his gaze. "What—"

He pulled out a condom and quickly rolled it on. Jenna closed her eyes and tried to find one drop of rationality inside her, but her blood was running too hot, her need too deep.

"We don't have to do this in the hall."

She opened her eyes and saw the passion in his gaze. She took a breath. "Yes," she said in that husky voice that was so unfamiliar to her. "We do."

His eyes darkened, and his nostrils flared. He lifted her slightly and positioned himself at the outer edge of her swollen femininity. "Look at me," he told her. "I want to watch you when I'm inside you."

Then he plunged inside her.

Although she'd expected it, wanted it, the invasion surprised her. Her body stretched to accommodate him. Her eyes widened.

Stan was alternately swearing and praying. "Oh, Jenna, you're so tight."

She still hadn't caught her breath. "It's not me. It's you." He shifted and thrust again, and she gave an involuntary shudder. "You're so big."

He swallowed and gave a rough chuckle. "No. It's you, but we've got better things to do than argue about it." With solid, fluid strokes he filled her again and again, taking her to the top again. All the while, he stared into her eyes, making her feel completely possessed by him.

Clinging to him, she felt herself intimately clench him again. She climaxed, and felt him tumble with her as he gave in to his release. The roaring in her head ceased, and what followed was like the stunned silence after a bomb had exploded. Suspended in time, they meshed bodies, minds and hearts as one. It was a moment of quiet, awesome wonder.

She was blown away, emotionally, physically. Her knees buckled, and she began to slide. Helplessly, she shook her head. "I'm sorry. I can't—"

In a movement so swift and sure it seemed like a reflex, he grasped her to him. "You're not going anywhere," he muttered.

He felt so warm, so solid. She glanced around, surprised to see that her hallway hadn't turned to rubble. His jeans and shirt were discarded on the floor on top of her dress. Even their clothes looked intimately joined. She gave a shaky sigh. "What do we do now?"

"I take you upstairs," he told her, pulling her up into his arms and moving toward the stairway. "And then we do what we just did all over again."

Jenna's heart turned over. She felt incredibly vulnerable. "Oh, wow," she said, wondering if she would survive.

Stan rubbed his lips over her forehead. "There's more, Jenna, so much more we can have together. You make me want it all at once."

And Jenna felt an alarming certainty that Stan had taken more than her body.

Stan carried her to bed and made love to her again and again. He'd always known once wouldn't be enough with Jenna. Although his body was sated, he was beginning to believe he'd never get enough. The notion wasn't completely comforting, but nothing in his life had ever felt so right. His choice to practice medicine approached it, as did his decision to return to Roanoke.

Nothing, however, had felt so right as taking Jenna Jean Anderson to bed and making love to her and holding her in his arms as she drifted off to sleep.

Thankful for a moment to study her when she was asleep, he looked his fill without distractions. Awake, Jenna was entirely too engaging. She demanded all his mental energy. For this silent moment when his body cooled, though, he stared down at the classic bone structure of her face, the fringe of her eyelashes shielding her eyes from him. He lightly rubbed his finger over the sculpted, yet feminine, curves of her jaw and chin that belied her stubborn nature.

The firm, gentle slope of one of her breasts was bared to him. In the past hours, he'd learned Jenna could be surprisingly shy about her nakedness. More modesty or vulnerability than self-consciousness, he thought, because she had nothing to be ashamed of when it came to her shape. Her body reminded him of a Thoroughbred. Long, lean and strong. Still her attitude made him feel protective. Clearly accustomed to sleeping alone, she lay on her side with her legs delicately folded together.

Stan wanted to change that. He wanted her long legs entwined with his, her arms wrapped around him. His gut tightened. The sight of her kiss-swollen lips aroused him again. He couldn't possibly want her again, he thought, but his mind and body argued the point.

The raw strength of how much he wanted her was dangerous. He'd never felt this way before. He narrowed his eyes, and a sliver of light dawned.

He wanted possession.

Possession of Jenna Jean Anderson. It would be no easy task to keep her, but when he was finished, her attorney's mind would have to concede that in this case possession was nine-tenths of the law.

Jenna awoke to the sensation of something tickling her nose. Her legs were trapped by something warm and heavy. Her eyelids felt as if someone had put two-pound weights on them. She wiggled her nose and squinted her eyes.

A moment passed and Jenna's eyes flew open as she felt the twinges and little aches from her love-making. She breathed in his scent, and every feminine nerve ending stood on end. Her face pressed into Stan's muscular chest, she moved her head back and saw his hard thigh over her legs. Her heart jumped.

With the sheets tangled at her ankles, she could see that he was naked, and so was she.

She wanted a few minutes to find her composure. Or her robe. She wanted a few minutes to catch her breath from the mind-blowing memories racing through her head. For all her toughness, Jenna had never figured out how to handle a morning-after with sophisticated ease. Part of the reason was because she hadn't had very many morning-afters.

Stan shifted and slipped his hand through her hair. Jenna bit back a moan of desperation. She was well and truly trapped.

She swallowed and slowly slid her legs from beneath his. "Excuse me," she whispered as she attempted to disentangle his fingers from her hair.

"Good morning, Jenna," he murmured in the voice that reduced her to honey. Then he ruined her getaway plan by rolling onto his back and pulling her on top of him.

His hair was mussed, his jaw shadowed with whiskers. His heavy-lidded eyes reminded her of a lion's. He should have looked rotten. Instead he looked unbearably sexy.

She swore under her breath.

His lips tilted slightly. "Does the counselor wake up cranky?"

Only when the counselor's life is *totally* out of control.

"Are you always this quiet in the morning?" he asked, turning his head slightly to look at her.

"Why aren't you uglier?" she asked, trying to turn the attention away from her. She ducked her head under his chin. "You're supposed to look much uglier in the morning."

Nuzzling her chin to bring it up, he chuckled. His hands roamed over her back and bottom. "Don't tell me you're shy."

Jenna closed her eyes. "Not shy. Just awkward." She tried to slide away. "I need to get ready for—"

He stopped her with a kiss. "It doesn't have to be awkward," Stan told her when he pulled back. "Once you get used to it, you might even like it."

She felt her heart bounce into her throat. "Get used to it," she repeated in a voice husky to her ears.

"Get used to seeing me in the morning," he said.

Refusing to believe the emotion she saw in his eyes, Jenna shook her head. "Ohh no. Don't do that. Don't even *suggest* you're interested in something long-term when you're not. This is when—"

He covered her lips with his thumb. "And what if I *am* interested in something long-term?"

Her stomach took a dip. Jenna blinked.

He watched her carefully. "Quiet again." He lifted his mouth to hers, then murmured, "Get used to seeing me in the morning."

Jenna was so rattled she had to smash every thought of Stan, which ended up happening entirely too often for her comfort. By lunch she was ready to hide in her office for a few minutes of peace and wits gathering.

As soon as she closed her office door, her phone rang. She almost didn't pick it up. Resigned, she lifted the receiver. "Hello," she said, then made a moue of disgust when someone knocked at her door. "Hold just a second, please.'' She put the receiver on her desk and opened the door to a man delivering flowers.

She lifted her hand to her throat in surprise. ''Flowers? For me?'' Jenna couldn't remember the last time she'd received flowers. Her heart bucked. Stan.

''Thank you,'' she said in a daze, then picked up the phone again. ''Hello.''

''Hi, beautiful Counselor,'' Stan said.

Jenna smiled. ''Hi to you.'' She sniffed one of the sweetheart roses.

''I'm supposed to go to a cocktail party for some of the new doctors Thursday night. Go with me.''

Jenna laughed. ''You give an order with one breath, send flowers with the next.''

A brief silence followed. ''Flowers?''

''Yes, they're beautiful. Little pink sweetheart roses, white carnations, baby's breath.'' She smelled them again. ''Thank you, Stan. It's been a long time since—'' A knock sounded at the door. ''Oops. I'm sorry. Could you wait just a second?''

Jenna quickly opened the door to another delivery man. This one wheeled two cases into her office. ''Two cases of champagne for Jenna Jean Anderson,'' the man said. ''Sign here.''

Feeling her blood sink to her feet, Jenna scrawled her signature, shoved the door shut and picked up the phone. ''You sent me champagne!''

''Yeah,'' Stan said. ''Enough to fill a freakin' bathtub. But I want to know who sent the flowers.''

He said the statement in a curious, friendly way, but she could feel the vibration of a competitive note sinking in. Frowning, Jenna opened the card and read it. She covered her face and thanked heaven no one was present to view her mortification. "Oops. It's from uh, Ned. What a surprise."

"I'm sure," Stan said, the competitive note growing stronger. "What did the note say?"

"Nothing really. Nothing significant."

"What did it say?"

She should tell him it was none of his business, but the cases of champagne seemed to accuse her. "Okay. Okay. It's nothing, but since you insist, he said, 'Dear Jenna, hope your headache's better. Hope these flowers brighten your day. Let's get together again soon. Regards, Ned.'" She took a quick breath. "See. I told you it was nothing."

"Headache?" Stan said. "You didn't mention a headache when I saw you Sunday night."

She scowled. "It went away."

"My healing touch."

Jenna sighed and smiled despite herself. "I guess so."

"Are you getting another headache now?"

"No. I think an anxiety attack is more likely." She heard footsteps outside her door. "I imagine everyone's curious why I got champagne, and I'll need to come up with a plausible explanation."

"You can tell them the doctor you made love with in your foyer last night is so grateful he wanted to send you something better than a puny, uninspired, unoriginal flower arrangement."

"I don't think so," Jenna murmured, wracking her brain for an alternate explanation.

"You'll go with me to the cocktail party," Stan said.

"You still haven't asked."

"I don't want you to say no."

His voice and words melted her. "Yes, I'll go."

"Good. And you'll let me watch you take a bath in that champagne," he said, his tone making her want him again.

She fanned herself with a notepad. "I'll have to *drink* a case of it first. I need to go. The natives outside my door are growing restless. Thank you for the champagne."

"Jenna Jean," Stan said, causing her to pause.

"Yes."

"I want you again."

Jenna sucked in a quick breath. "Stop," she said desperately. "You're messing with my mind."

Stan chuckled, low and dirty. "Oh, Your Majesty, I'm going to mess with a lot more than your mind. Don't worry about needing another case of champagne. I'll bring it tonight."

Nine

Stan was in no mood for champagne Monday evening. When he learned Jordan's brother hadn't been home in three days, Stan was ready to hit the ceiling. He called Jenna to make his apologies, but she drew the story out of him and promised to drive to his apartment immediately.

To rid himself of his excess energy, he joined Jordan on the basketball court.

"Why didn't you call me?" Stan asked as he took a jump shot.

Jordan grabbed the rebound and shrugged. "No big deal. He's stayed out before."

"Weren't you a little afraid?"

Jordan shook his head. "Nah." Stan blocked him as he tried to dribble toward the basket. "I don't like the gunshots much though."

Stan felt his blood boil. "Wouldn't you like to live somewhere else?"

"Where? This is the best apartment my brother can afford." He sneaked around Stan and made a hook shot.

The idea that had been brewing in Stan's mind came to the forefront again. Jordan was a good kid, and Stan cared about him. He cared about him enough to want to take care of him, but he resisted the urge to broach the subject with Jordan. He wanted to discuss it with Jenna first. He wanted to talk it over with Jenna because she was a lawyer, Stan told himself, but deep down he knew there were other reasons.

"You wanna stay here tonight?" he asked Jordan, and watched the relief cross the boy's face.

Clearly fighting any sign of vulnerability, he shrugged. "It's okay with me if it's okay with you."

Stan nodded, and noticed Jenna pull into the parking lot. "We'll call one of your neighbors and ask them to leave a message. Here comes Jenna. C'mon inside when it gets dark. Okay?"

Jordan grinned. "Okay, Mom."

Stan chuckled and swatted him. "Smart-aleck kid."

"Yes. I'm sure Jordan was a nice, well-mannered young man until you influenced him," Jenna said as she walked toward them. Dressed in casual shorts and a pullover top, she still managed to look neat and untouchable. The image always made Stan's fingers itch to mess her up. She had a smart mouth and a sexy walk. Sometimes he wondered if she had been specially designed to make him feel like a loaded weapon.

He slid a glance toward Jordan to find the boy grinning at her. Poor kid probably had a crush on her half as bad as his own. "Enough insults, Queen Jenna, what's in the bag?"

Jenna looked down her nose at him. "Wait your turn."

"My turn," he said, moving beside her to slip his arm around her waist.

She opened the paper bag and gave Jordan two cookies.

"When it comes to you, Jenna Jean, my turn is *always*," Stan told her, and held out his hand.

"Ha!" she said, sticking out her chin as she slipped away from him. "Better watch out, Stan*ley*. Your arrogance is showing." In true Cherry Lane fighter mode, she made it sound like his underwear was showing.

Stan felt her challenge like a sensual kick. One way or another, the woman never failed to get a rise out of him. He went after her, scooping her up in his arms. "*This* is the way you get cookies," he called to Jordan, who was staring at them in baffled amusement.

"That's singular. Cookie," she told him heatedly. "There's only one left, you neanderthal."

He tossed her a mock-indignant look. "One! You gave him *two!*"

Jordan quickly popped the rest of his second cookie in his mouth and gave a crumbly smile. "All gone," he said around the cookie, then turned back to dribbling the basketball.

"Smart kid," Jenna said as Stan carried her to his

apartment. "He ate the evidence. You can put me down now."

"Not until I get my cookie," Stan told her, liking the weight of her in his arms. She felt good there...right.

Jenna gave a put-upon sigh and handed over the bag. "Some boys *never* grow up."

Stan thought of Jordan's brother and lost his sense of humor. He set Jenna on her feet. "That's what I need to talk to you about. Boys who take their time growing up."

She seemed to sense his change of mood. "You're angry."

"That's just for starters," he said, opening his door. "I want to sue for custody."

Jenna rubbed her forehead and sighed, following him inside the apartment. "That can be a long, drawn-out process. It can get messy."

"I don't care about the mess. There's a good kid out there who has *no* adult watching out for him. He gives a tough-guy impression, but it doesn't take much to see he's scared and alone." Hearing his voice rise in volume, he took a deep breath and turned away from her. "I'm not yelling at you."

"I know," she said, trailing her fingers down his arm in a motion that soothed him at the same time it made him acutely aware of the strength of his desire for her. "You're yelling because you care."

He turned around to meet her gaze. "I can do this."

She gave him an assessing look that lasted mere seconds before she nodded. "Our office doesn't handle adoptions, but there might be an easier way to handle this. Do you know if Jordan has any living relatives?''

"None that are interested."

"Have you met his brother?"

"No," he said, feeling the burn invade his stomach again. He grabbed an empty soda can from the counter and crumpled it. "Tim's never been around when I dropped Jordan at the apartment."

Jenna narrowed her eyes thoughtfully. "I think I remember one of the intake guys at the court talking about how quickly a change of custody went through when the guardian agreed. Maybe if you talked with Tim, you could show him how it would benefit both him *and* Jordan if Jordan lived with you." She looked at the smashed soda can. "You'll need to choose your words carefully, though. And you need to discuss it with Jordan. See how he feels about it.

"Even though Tim isn't doing a good job of taking care of Jordan right now, he's still his brother. Somewhere down the line, they'll both be adults, and that tie will be very important to them." She paused. "If you can make it okay for both Tim and Jordan for you to become Jordan's guardian, it will be easier for everyone."

He took her hand in his and tugged her closer. "How'd you get to be so smart?"

Her lips tilted slightly. "I was always smart."

"Always a show-off. You think I'm crazy," he said.

She hesitated and slowly shook her head. "No. I admire you."

Stan felt his heart swell at her words and the soft expression in her eyes. Her unique mix of calling him on the carpet if she disagreed with him and affirming him right where he needed it was taking him into deep water. Where he'd never been. He sifted his fingers through her hair. "After I talk this over with Jordan, how am I going to gently persuade his brother he's doing a rotten job and I can do a helluva lot better?"

She smiled. "You might want to reconsider your word choice, and take them both out to dinner."

He held her against him. "You could come with us," he whispered.

"Nuh-uh. With his court experience, I don't think Tim would be comfortable sitting across from the assistant commonwealth attorney."

He slid his hands beneath her shirt. Her skin was soft and warm. "Jenna, I want to make love to you."

He saw her eyes darken with passion and a tinge of regret. "We can't. You have a teenager who will be bounding through the door any minute."

"Ouch." He hugged her tightly.

Jenna toyed with the hair on the back of his neck. He loved the way she touched him.

"This could put a crimp in your love life, Dr. S&M," she said.

He drew back slightly to study her. "A crimp in my relationship with you?"

She gave him a surprised look. "No, but I'm sure you'll have to make some adjustments."

"Jordan's used to a long lead rope, so he won't want me hovering. I'm only a beep away."

"No more all-nighters," Jenna pointed out.

"Unless I arrange for him to stay with someone responsible and reliable."

"Sounds like you have a plan."

"I do, Jenna," Stan said. *I'm gonna get you.
I'm gonna keep you.*

"I can't believe you've fallen for Stanley Michaels," Maddie said, shaking her head. When the waiter peeked around the corner, she pointed at her glass for a refill of her beer. "You couldn't stand him."

Uncomfortable, Jenna took a long drink of soda, wishing it were whiskey. She wasn't at ease about her involvement with Stan. Not at all. "I wouldn't say I've *fallen,*" she corrected Maddie.

"Well, what would you call it? You let him stay with you all night, then gave him free advice—"

"Options, not advice." Maddie was making her nervous.

Maddie gave a dismissive wave of her hand. "And you're not the least bit turned off by the fact that he's going to have a teenager hanging around a lot of the time. This, from the woman who swore she would never date a man with children."

"Jordan's a nice kid," she said, trying not to be defensive. "He deserves a chance."

"Uh-huh," Maddie said. "Plus you haven't stopped talking about Stan since you got here."

Jenna bit her lip. "I can talk about other things. How are Davey and Joshua?"

"Fine, except Davey's teething, so he's occasionally miserable." She smiled. "It's okay, Jenna. You had to fall sometime. I'm just surprised it's Stanley."

Me, too. "It's gotta be temporary," she muttered. "We're not well suited."

"Oh, I don't know. I think there's a sort of divine

justice to it. You're a lawyer. He's a doctor.'' She batted her eyes demurely. ''Anal retentive meets God complex.''

Jenna scowled. ''You're evil.''

''You love me.''

Jenna sighed. ''You're right. I do.''

Maddie's expression softened. ''What about you? Do you love Stan?''

Jenna's stomach clenched and her mind rebelled. ''I can't,'' she said, but a still, small voice inside her said she could.

''Why couldn't you?'' Maddie asked, all wide-eyed concern.

''Well, he's too—''

''Good-looking? Stan has filled out in all the right places.''

A visceral image of Stan's naked body sliced into her mind. She took a quick sip of her soda and shook off the intimate picture. She began again. ''Stan is too—''

''Intelligent,'' Maddie said, nodding. ''He's always had his mental Wheaties.'' Before Jenna could say anything, Maddie went on. ''Plus he's obviously gotten his act together since he's a doctor.'' She shrugged. ''With all that going for him, he's probably a dud in bed.''

Jenna's breath hung in her throat.

Maddie met her gaze, understanding lighting her brown eyes. ''That bad, huh? And when I say that bad, I mean that good.''

Jenna nodded stiffly, playing with her drink.

''Did he call the next day?''

She nodded again.

"Did he send flowers?"

Jenna shook her head and gave a breathless chuckle. "Champagne. Two crates of champagne."

Maddie looked impressed. "Now, *that* is classy. Classy and sexy. Jenna," she said, "I can't say I'm sad you're involved with him. I was beginning to wonder if you would be the first woman to make medical history by getting her virginity back."

Jenna shook her head. "I don't know about this. It seems like he's always got women chasing him."

Maddie made a face. "That could be a bummer. You probably wonder if you'll be shooing them away with flyswatters the rest of your life."

The thought made her feel unsure. It made her question her feminine appeal, a secret vulnerable point for Jenna. So secret she'd never discussed it with even her closest friends. "I always thought I'd get involved with a calm, conservative sort of man...who wouldn't have women throwing themselves at him."

"If he's hooked on you, it won't matter if every female in the state of Virginia throws herself at him."

"Maybe," Jenna said as the waiter delivered their food.

Maddie tilted her head to one side, and Jenna could practically see an antennae sprout from her. "Maybe? You've had your share of admirers even though you haven't given most of them the time of day. You're pretty, extremely intelligent, very successful—"

Although Jenna was studying her food, she felt Maddie's surprised stare. She didn't know why, but she felt twelve years old again, skinny, all arms, legs, braces and stringy hair. A rush of feelings she'd always run from hit her like a pounding wave, and this time she couldn't jump out of the way.

"Jenna, you're the most confident woman I know."

Jenna nodded and stuck her fork into the rice on her plate. "I am confident about a lot of things—my job, my ability to handle most everyday situations, and relating with my peers."

"But not men," Maddie said bluntly. "I always thought the reason you didn't date much was because you thought you didn't have enough time, or you didn't find someone worth the trouble."

Feeling vulnerable and not liking it, Jenna put her fork down. "That's part of my reasoning, but I always wondered—or doubted I'd be able to hold a man." She swore under her breath. "Do we have to talk about this?"

"Yes," Maddie said emphatically. "It's about time, isn't it? Let me get this straight. Most women get past their insecurities by trying to please men, but you bluffed your way past yours by acting confident and as if you could care less."

Still uncomfortable, Jenna barely resisted the urge to twitch. "Confidence can hide a multitude of fears and insecurities. It can almost hide runs in panty hose."

"What you need to do is get out your bag of womanly wiles and—"

"I don't have womanly wiles," Jenna told her.

"Yes, you do. Trust me. They're in there somewhere. You need to pull them out and play with them a little bit."

Jenna lifted her eyebrows skeptically. "Play with them?"

Maddie smiled. "Yeah. And you've got the perfect man to play with. Stan."

Jenna shook her head. "Oh, I don't know, Maddie." She covered her eyes. "I see complete embarrassment and humiliation in my future."

Maddie made a tsking sound. "I never thought I'd see the day when Jenna Jean Anderson was a *wimp*."

The word was like ice water in her face. Jenna stared at Maddie. "That's really low."

Maddie shrugged and took a bite of her burger. "I call it the way I see it."

"Besides, there's one major requirement that Stan doesn't fulfill."

"What's that?"

"He's not controllable."

At the cocktail party the following night, Stan greeted her with a kiss, in front of all the other doctor gods. "You look great. Sorry I couldn't pick you up. I had an emergency. Thanks for meeting me here."

Her stomach flipped at the sight of him. "No problem." She lifted her hand to his damp hair. "Just out of the shower?"

"Yeah." His lips tilted in a too-sexy grin. "Wish you could have been with me."

"I'm sure that would have gone over great with the rest of the staff," Jenna said. "Where's Jordan?"

Stan's expression gentled. "He's at his brother's. I talked with him, and he wants to think about it."

"Good." Jenna nodded. "It's a lot to think about

it. I'm sure it means something to him that you're just a phone call away."

"Yeah. Hey, let me get you a drink and introduce you around."

He brought her champagne, and with his hand at her waist he began to take her around the room to various doctors and administrative directors, wives and husbands, and a few nurses. He teased her and made pleasantries with his colleagues, then whispered explicit promises in her ear. With his constant touch and secret words, he kept Jenna at a slow simmer all evening.

Most of his colleagues were very warm to her, but Jenna could sense that a few of them were scrutinizing her.

She left Stan's side for a moment to set her plate down, when a pharmacist crossed paths with her. "When I heard Stan was bringing a woman to the party tonight, I didn't expect anyone like you."

Jenna tensed, but noticed the woman was smiling. "You didn't," she replied in a noncommittal tone.

"Well, he's known for fluffy women," the woman said.

"Fluffy," Jenna said, although she had a sinking feeling she understood what the pharmacist was saying.

"Yes. You know. Fluffy hair, fluffy names, fluffy brains. You're different."

"Thank you," she said, and returned the woman's smile as she left. "I think."

Unfortunately the pharmacist wasn't the only person to make comments on what a surprise Jenna was. As she drove home with Stan following her in his car, the assorted comments rolled through her mind. *You're different. How in the world did you two get together?* The one that did the most damage was murmured behind her back. It dredged up her secret fears and vulnerability.

It'll never last. She's not his type.

Ten

"Bath time," Stan said with a wicked glint in his eye as he lifted two bottles of champagne. "We're in luck. They're already chilled."

Jenna's heart squeezed as she leaned against her front door. She thought she had lost him a couple of miles before she'd arrived at her house because she hadn't seen him behind her anymore. Combined with the comment she'd overheard, it had made *her* feel lost. It was a new and terrible feeling.

She glanced at the champagne and shook her head. "This is not going to happen."

"Such a negative attitude," he said, and swaggered past her. "You must've gotten that on the way home. You were smiling until we left the party."

"You were with me then," she murmured, closing the door.

Gazing at her thoughtfully, he moved closer. "I can do that again."

Jenna felt the tug of her doubt and the pull of Stan's sensual persuasion. She blew a strand of her hair from her face. "I made some cookies. Want one?" She walked toward the kitchen.

He snagged her arm and pulled her back against him. "C'mon, Queen Jenna Jean. What's going on inside that pretty head of yours?"

"Nothing," she said, feeling her heartbeat get away from her.

Stan chuckled. "Lousy lie. There's not a minute that goes by that your brain isn't clicking at superspeed. Tell the truth."

"The whole truth and nothing but the truth," she said. "I'd rather give you a cookie."

Stan narrowed his eyes and turned her around to meet his gaze. "Talk to me."

Jenna sighed and dipped her head. "It's nothing. Just something I overheard at the cocktail party."

"What was it?"

"You're not going to quit, are you?"

He shook his head. "Spill it."

"It's nothing. Most of the people I met were very nice. A few commented on how I wasn't your usual flavor of the month."

Anger slid through his veins. "Their words?"

"Close." She shrugged, then met his gaze. He hated the doubt he saw in her eyes. "One said I wouldn't last. I wasn't your type."

His chest tightened. "And?"

"And it reminded me of the differences between us. It made me think."

He gritted his teeth, but kept his tone calm. He felt like smashing the champagne bottles against the wall. "What did it make you think?"

She hesitated, still meeting his gaze. Something about the way she stood and the expression on her face told him this was hard for her to say. He felt an odd pang.

"I guess I wonder when you'll get tired of me."

Stunned, all he could do was stare. "You've got to be kidding."

She gave a little shake of her head. "I'm not." She lifted her hand to stop him before he started. "Think about it, Stan. I'm not at all like the kind of woman you usually date."

"We've been over this before. It's a good thing you're not like the other women I've dated," Stan said, wanting to eradicate her doubt.

"Possibly," she conceded. "I hate to sound sexist, but if women were ice cream flavors, I would be vani—"

"A double-crunch bar," he immediately said and set down the champagne.

Her brows furrowed in confusion, she looked at him blankly. "You've lost me."

"I better not have," he said, and swung her up into his arms, pleased she was distracted enough not to protest. "We've just gotten started. A double-crunch looks like a regular vanilla bar covered with a choc-olate coating. When you eat your way past the vanilla to the middle, you find a fudge center."

She looked at him as if he were crazy. "Still lost."

He carried her into the den and set her down on

the sofa. "You look like a classic on the outside, but there's a great surprise on the inside."

"You're not suggesting that I'm soft on the inside." Her blue eyes were wide with indignation.

He leaned down to press his lips against hers, sliding his tongue into her mouth to taste and take her. When he pulled back, he could practically feel the steam rise from his head. Jenna wore a sexually dazed look that spiked his temperature another degree.

"Very soft," he told her. "You try to hide it with a tough external layer, but I've been all the way to the center, and I want more," he murmured, and rubbed his jaw against her soft silky hair. "I won't get tired of you."

"How can you be sure?" she whispered.

His chest tightened again. The doubt in her voice was still there, and Stan saw it as a threat. He wanted her, all of her, including her trust. It was more than want. It felt like *need.* His male defenses bucked at the notion, but Stan couldn't deny how important Jenna was becoming to him.

"I know myself better than I ever have. I know what I like and what I don't like. I know what I want," he told her. "And what I want is you."

Her eyes deepened with vulnerability, and it made him want to hold her close. His heart squeezed tight. Who would have known that smart, tough Jenna Jean could be so tender? Who would have known she would affect him so much? The truth burst across his mind like fireworks, shocking and spectacular. She was the magical, elusive combination of Woman he'd been looking for his entire life.

And he'd first met her in his backyard. She'd nailed

him when a crowd of neighborhood kids were playing tag. She didn't know it, but she'd nailed him again.

He remembered Joey, one of his buddies, ribbing him about when he was going to *get* Jenna Jean. The time had come.

"Keep your seat and let me get some glasses for this champagne. Which cabinet?"

She hesitated at his change of gears. "Second on the left. But—"

She tried to stand, but he gently pressed her back down. "It's okay. Keep your seat."

He returned with the champagne.

Jenna gave him a sideways look. "You're not going to try to get me drunk, are you?"

"Me?" he asked with all the innocence he could muster.

"You're the one holding the champagne."

He grinned and handed her a half-full glass. "Not anymore." Sitting beside her, he toyed with her hair. "I don't want to get you drunk, just relaxed."

"I'm not getting in a bathtub full of champagne. You can't make me," she told him, taking a sip. Her tone was defiant, but she gave herself away by curling her head against his hand.

Stan bit back a grin. "Tell me who you fried in court today."

She rolled her eyes. "You don't want to hear. It'll put you to sleep."

He ditched his jacket and tie, then pulled her onto his lap. She felt good. Her breasts pressed against his chest, making him wonder what kind of bra she wore and how long it would take him to get it off. "I've always liked a good bedtime story," he murmured.

She gave a slight shake of her head. "Okay, but remember you asked. Once upon a time, the Roanoke City Police set up a speed-limit surveillance—"

"Speed trap," Stan said in disgust, and topped off her glass of champagne.

"It's their job to enforce the law. Speed limits are also a safety issue."

"And the tickets provide an easy source of revenue."

Jenna paused. "Are you *sure* you want to know what I did in court today?"

"Of course," Stan said.

Jenna lifted a skeptical eyebrow. "The Roanoke City Police caught quite a few persons exceeding the speed limit. Some of these people were not pleased, so they decided to protest the charges."

Stan made a face. "So you had to listen to a bunch of whiners with stupid excuses about why they were speeding today."

Jenna nodded. "One woman was late picking up her children from child-care. One man was afraid he wouldn't make his dental appointment. Another insisted the arresting officer's radar equipment was wrong. The one that took the cake, however, was the man who told the court he and his wife were trying to get pregnant. Apparently her temperature indicated the need for—" she hesitated, clearly searching for the right term "—action, so he rushed home from the office."

Stan grinned. He liked this. He liked having Jenna in his lap, sharing her day with him. He could get used to it. He would like it even better if he could get her out of her dress. "What did the judge do?"

"He let him off with a warning."

He pressed his thumb between her ribs in a teasing manner. "Did you object?"

Jenna wiggled and shook her head. "Nope. Now tell me about your day. How many women hit on you?"

Ignoring her question, he gave in to his desire to take her mouth in a long, full kiss. She tasted of champagne and sweetness, and her scent ran through him like a rush of adrenaline. He couldn't get enough of her.

He reluctantly pulled back, she looked at him with a dazed expression. "You're trying to distract me from my question."

"Did it work?"

"Almost." When he lowered his head to kiss her again, she ducked. "Uh-uh. How many women hit on you today?"

He started to deny, then remembered a minor emergency he'd taken care of this morning. "Just one," he said, and swallowed a grin at the way Jenna's eyes narrowed ever so slightly. "Long, blond hair, blue eyes. She made an indecent request."

She did a double take she tried to hide. "What was that?" she asked in a calm voice before she took a healthy swallow of champagne.

Damn, she was good, Stan thought in admiration. "No wonder you're so good in court," he told her. "You know exactly how to use your voice to keep the emotion out of it when you need to."

"Why do you say that?" she asked, mildly curious.

"Because you're jealous as hell."

A touch of anger tightened her mouth. "No. I'm not."

He tugged at her bottom lip with his fingers. "Are, too."

"Am not."

"So it doesn't bother you that a blond, blue-eyed patient of mine made an indecent proposal today?"

She took a deep breath. "It *might* bother me a little, but that doesn't necessarily constitute jealousy."

Stan grinned. "We're arguing semantics, darlin', and since you do it for a living, I'll stop while I'm ahead."

A brief silence followed and Jenna shifted in his lap. "Well, finish the story. What did she want you to do?"

Stan topped off her champagne again and began to stroke her leg. "She had broken a finger, and she wanted me to kiss it."

"Kiss it!" Jenna stared at him, then realization dawned and she shot him an accusing look. "How old was she?"

"Four, but—"

Sparks flew from her eyes. "That was low and dirty."

"I can get lower and dirtier." He nuzzled her neck and slid his hand over her thigh.

He felt something cool rush down his back, and Jenna jumped from his lap. He stiffened, staring in amazement at her empty glass. "You dumped your champagne down my back!"

She looked just as stunned at herself. She put her hand to her throat and looked at the empty glass as if it were an alien. "Omigod, you're still doing it to me."

Seizing the opportunity, Stan stood and ditched his shirt. Her eyes fell over his chest like a warm wave before she looked away. "Doing what?" he asked.

"Making me do irrational things. When we were kids, I bit you so hard you needed stitches. I made love with you in my foyer. Now I'm dumping champagne on you."

She looked so genuinely distressed that his heart softened yet again toward her. Drawing her into his arms, he tried to humor her. "It's terrible, isn't it?"

"Yes, it is," she said, then frowned as he unfastened the zipper of her dress. "What are you doing?"

"Helping you out of your dress." He let it fall to the floor and thanked his lucky stars she'd skipped nylons tonight.

"But—"

"Fair's fair," he said, drawing her against him again as she stood in her bra and panties and nothing else. His temperature surged, and he felt a tightening in his groin. "Jenna, can you tell me how the assistant commonwealth attorney ended up with a body that could stop a freight train?"

She opened his mouth to dispute him, then closed it. "It could?"

He slid his hands over her bottom and pulled her against his crotch. "Oh, yes. Honey, you feel so good all over it's almost a sin for you to wear clothes."

"You'd have me nude all the time?" she murmured as he skimmed his lips over her shoulder.

Just the thought of having intimate access to her body all the time made him so hard it hurt. "Yes."

"I think I'd have a tough time in court," she managed a shade breathlessly, and began to run her hands over his torso and lower.

Stan gave a rough chuckle. His self-control strained, he wondered if he would eat her alive. He unfastened her bra and caressed her breasts. Her nipples were tight buds. He wanted them against his chest, in his mouth, glancing his thighs as her mouth performed all kinds of intimate pleasuring. He moaned as she slid her hand inside his pants and stroked him intimately.

He rubbed her nipple with his thumb at the same time she fondled him. He felt as if he would explode.

"You didn't finish your story," Jenna said as her brain began to melt with the rest of her. "Did you kiss the blue-eyed blonde?"

Stan nodded, but he was clearly distracted. He swore when she arched against him. Jenna didn't understand why her body felt as if it had been made for his, why she responded to him the way she did. It was much more than physical, though. He had her attention mentally and emotionally, too.

Her heart felt too full for her chest. "You know, you can be a nice guy," she told him in a husky voice, her mouth against his.

He kissed her again, his mouth and body hungry for her. When he pulled back, he said, "You sound surprised."

"I am. You keep surprising me."

"I like surprising you," he said with an expression in his gaze that would rival the devil's. He looked like a man hungry enough to eat one assistant commonwealth attorney.

A thrill raced through her.

Shifting slightly, he hooked his hand around his still-full glass of champagne behind him on the table. He took a sip and lifted the glass to her lips for a drink.

It was a sexual gesture. *Take my wine.*

Take me.

Her heart pounding, Jenna lowered her head to sip.

He shifted his hand slightly and sent the cool, gold liquid spilling down the front of her.

Jenna gasped, more in surprise, than outrage. His eyes were more aroused than ever. "Payback?"

"In a way," he conceded.

She felt his gaze. He was watching the way the droplets clung to the tips of her breasts. Her nipples tightened to swollen, achy nubs.

"It's more my way of getting you one step closer to the bathtub." He lowered his mouth to sip at her neck, and she shuddered. "Don't worry," he told her, skimming his mouth down to her breasts. "You won't need a towel."

The sensation of his warm tongue, combined with the cool liquid on her sensitized skin, made her tremble.

"Cold?" he asked, closing his mouth around a nipple and sucking.

The sight was too erotic for words. She closed her eyes for a second to get her bearings. She couldn't find them. "Cold," she managed huskily. "And hot."

He chuckled slightly as he slid his tongue across the valley between her breasts to her other nipple. "Oh, Jenna, if someone could bottle this taste, he could make a million."

Overwhelmed, Jenna swallowed at the knot of emotion in her throat. "Champagne *is* bottled."

He shook his head, then looked at her with eyes that could have burned her to cinders. "They can't bottle you."

Too much. She felt too much at once. Pleasure, fear, joy, disbelief. "Don't do this. Please don't."

His face twisting in confusion, he lifted his head, but kept his arms around her. "You don't like it?"

"No," she said. "I mean yes." She bit her lip and was appalled to feel the threat of tears. "Just please don't mislead me. Don't say things you don't mean. Don't make me feel like the most special woman in the world to you if I'm not."

"And what if you are?"

"If you keep saying it and keep acting like it, I might start to believe you."

He lifted her hand to his mouth and kissed it. "Maybe that's what I'm hoping, Jenna Jean."

Jenna was afraid to believe, but with each tender kiss, each fervent stroke, each intent look, he held her heart as surely as his arms held her body.

Hours passed while he made love to her and she made love to him. Though she wasn't sure she wanted to, she opened up to him and felt a wonder she'd never felt before. She'd never known there could be such beauty in a simple touch, such aching need in a glance. She'd never dreamed she could feel so much all at once.

Eleven

With Stan's arm wrapped snugly around her, Jenna curled naked and content against his side. She was so sated and happy she could only sigh.

"You did it again," he said.

"What's that?" she asked, lifting her head to look at him. She played with the dimple in his chin.

"Sighed. Am I boring you?"

"Need a little ego food?" She smiled. "I'm sighing because I'm completely satisfied. Happy?"

"Yeah." He stole a kiss, then looked at her through sexy slitted eyes. "But your mind's headed for warp speed, so tell me what's going on inside there," he said, sliding his fingers through her hair.

"I'm just wondering a little," she murmured.

"Oh, no."

She lightly punched him. "It's not all bad."

"Okay then share, Queen Jenna."

"I was thinking that you took care of one of my fantasies tonight."

"Just one?"

She laughed and shook her head. "Still need more ego food? You took care of my champagne fantasy tonight."

"Not completely. I still have to get you in the tub."

She put her fingers over his mouth. "Close enough. I realize most of your sexual fantasies have probably been fulfilled," she said dryly. "But, Dr. Studmuffin, do you have any secret wishes or fantasies?"

He was quiet for a moment, looking at the ceiling, then turning his gaze on Jenna. "The closest anyone has ever come to asking me that question was when my parents asked me what I wanted for Christmas or my birthday."

The tenderness in his eyes tugged at her. "Well, do you?"

He hesitated, then nodded. "Yeah." He wrapped both arms around her and drew her into his embrace. "A psychologist might say this stems from my being an only child."

"What does Stan say?"

"Stan might agree."

With her cheek resting on his chest where his heart beat, Jenna couldn't see his face, but she could feel him looking at her. "I want to belong," he said in a low voice. "I want to connect so completely with another person that I am almost a necessity for them and they're almost a necessity for me."

Her heart tightened, and her throat grew thick with

emotion. With each moment she spent with him, it felt as if the stakes were getting higher.

"You're quiet," he said, gently tugging a strand of her hair. "Did I put you to sleep again?"

Jenna shook her head. "I was just thinking about your wish."

"And?"

"It sounds like it could be risky to need and be needed that much."

"It could," he conceded, then shifted slightly so he could look at her. She felt as if his gaze cut all the way to her center. "If it's the right woman and the right man, it will be so natural it will be hard to fight it."

Losing herself in his eyes, she took a careful breath. "Like sliding," she murmured.

"Down a sliding board."

"Or into quicksand."

His lips twitched and he lifted her hand to weave his fingers through hers. "The difference is you don't do it alone." He brought her hand to his lips and kissed it. "I do have one other fantasy," he told her, a wicked glint lighting his eyes. "It involves the Mill Mountain Star."

Jenna blinked. A Roanoke landmark, the Mill Mountain Star was an eighty-eight-and-one-half-foot-tall neon light that had been erected over forty years ago. It was one of the biggest artificial stars ever built, and it had given Roanoke the nickname Star City of the South.

Jenna's mind whirled with possibilities. Surely this wasn't a sexual fantasy, she told herself. "You want to climb it. Right?"

He shook his head slowly, and she could read his gaze as clearly as the newspaper. "Now that I've told you, you have to make it come true."

"I didn't see that in the fine print."

His mouth tugged into a half grin. "I dare you."

Jenna tossed him a disapproving look. "Don't even try that with me."

"Chicken," he said, boldly sliding his hands over her breasts and lower.

Her heart skipped a beat. "It won't work."

"I dare you." He slipped his hand between her thighs.

"You can't make me," she said breathlessly, but when he took her mouth again, he made her forget what they were arguing about.

Over the following weeks, Jenna realized she had slid to the point that she was now sunk. She saw Stan nearly every day, and they talked frequently on the phone. Her ankle improved so that she could give both Stan and Jordan a run for their money on the basketball court.

Although it had gone against his grain, Stan didn't pressure Jordan, because it was clear the teen's loyalties were torn. On several occasions Stan even took Jordan and his brother out for dinner to help the communication.

Stan and Jenna had discussed Jordan's situation many times, and they understood that if Jordan wanted to live with Stan, it would be a process not likely achieved overnight, and Jordan would still want to maintain ties with his brother.

It was tricky, but it was worth it.

It was tricky loving Dr. Stan Michaels, but Jenna was finding it worth the risk. With Stan around, talking, touching and teasing her, she didn't mind walking the balance beam quite so much.

Loving Stan like she did changed her outlook. She laughed more. She noticed the sky more. She felt more, even when she wasn't with him.

Her deep feelings for him inspired her to do something special for his upcoming birthday. A surprise to take care of his wish to belong. When she started trying to find members of *The Bad Boys Club,* she knew she'd gotten in over her head, but contacting the now grown-up boys became a quest, a challenge. A dare.

"You're going to have to have that phone surgically removed," he told her as he walked into her house the night before his birthday.

Determined not to get caught, Jenna made a face at him. "I hope that helps," she told the person on the phone, who was going to bake Stan's birthday cake. "I'll talk to you tomorrow if you need something else. Okay? Uh-huh. Bye, now." She hung up the phone.

He kissed her, and Jenna felt the now-familiar sliding sensation inside her. "I like the way you blew them off for me," he said. "Work again?"

"It's very busy since one of the attorneys quit," she hedged and put her arms around his neck. "How was your day?"

"Challenging," he said. "A woman fell down her steps, and I had to put in a pin and four screws."

Jenna winced. "Ouch."

"I told her she would always have a great excuse for setting off metal detectors."

"Did she hit you?"

He grinned. "No. She's not like you. What are you giving me for my birthday?"

Jenna faked a blank expression. "Your birthday? Is your birthday soon?"

He shot her a dark look. "Stop teasing, Queenie. I know you've got a mind like a steel trap. You know my birthday's tomorrow. I have suggestions for what you can give me."

She shook her head and made a tsking sound. "My, my. How demanding. Just what I'd expect from an only child. What do you want for your birthday, Dr. Studmuffin?"

"I'm tired of living in my apartment."

Jenna nodded. "You've been looking for a house."

He played with a lock of her hair. "I've decided where I want to live."

Her heart never failed to turn over when he touched her. A month ago she would have scorned the feelings. Today she relished them. She sighed. "Where's that?"

"Here."

Jenna's brain stalled for a full moment. She felt him regarding her thoughtfully and tried to find her equilibrium.

"I want to move in with you for my birthday," he told her, and the hunger in his gaze grabbed her in her midsection. "What do you think?"

She cleared her throat and wished she could clear her mind as easily. "Well, it's not along the same lines as the tie I was looking at."

"Let me move in. I want to be with you all the time." His voice was low and husky.

Jenna's heart twisted and she pulled back. "I'm going to have to think about this. You should, too. What about Jordan?"

"I thought I might save him for Halloween or Thanksgiving."

Jenna groaned. "You're moving too fast."

He nodded. "I understand. You can let me know at dinner tomorrow night."

Alarm and amusement battled inside her. She looked at him helplessly. "That's less than twenty-four hours."

He reached for her and she sidestepped him. "I always said you were quick. I had a helluva time trying to nail you when we played tag." He feinted to the left and caught her when she turned the other way.

She laughed weakly as he pulled her against him. "Is this some kind of macho one-upmanship?"

"No. I just want to get you back."

She shook her head and play-pounded his chest.

"I'm not letting you slide off the subject that easily. You should let me move in with you. You would like having a man around the house."

Still playing with him, she met his gaze. "Everytime you would leave your socks and underwear on the floor, I would have flashbacks to the sound of my mother fussing at my dad and brothers."

His eyes widened in mock innocence. "Me? Leave socks and underwear on the floor?"

"Plus, you would be pushy, and you would eat all my cookies."

"I would be your resident quality-control expert."

Jenna groaned and dipped her head against his chest.

"I want to be with you. All the time."

She felt his chest expand as if he were holding his breath and sensed this was an important moment for him. Her heart hammered against her rib cage, and she slowly lifted her gaze to his.

His eyes were clear with certainty and conviction, his expression so powerfully resolute it shook her.

"I love—"

She instinctively covered his lips with her fingers before he could finish. Moved and terrified, she began to tremble. "Don't say that unless you truly, truly mean it," she whispered.

She swallowed hard. This was one of the last barriers she had to completely belonging to Stan, and Jenna feared that once she belonged to him, she would never be free again. "Please. I'm not sure I could take it, if we went our separate ways after you said that."

Stan nodded, and just a hint of tenderness filtered into his gaze. "You," he said against her fingertips. "I love you, Jenna Jean Anderson. And if I have my way, I'm gonna make you love me, too."

He lowered his head to kiss her, and Jenna hid the tears in her eyes by closing them. Her heart was well and truly caught. Stan already had his way. He just didn't know it.

Despite the fact that Jenna technically had no time to think the following day, her mind kept flitting back to the idea of Stan moving in with her. It was surprisingly easy to visualize him living with her, what life would be like. Everytime she thought of it, her stomach took a dip, but by the end of the day she felt an overwhelming sense of rightness. It was almost as if they were destined to be together. She found herself grabbing hold of all the possibilities she could have with Stan more and more throughout the day.

By the time she left work, Jenna was practically buzzing with anticipation. It was time for Stan's surprise party, and she would be on a tight schedule for the next few hours. He had given her the keys and asked her to meet him at his apartment because his patient load had been heavy recently and he wasn't sure he would be able to leave on time. So Jenna had instructed the guests to park on the opposite side of the complex and meet at his apartment. With all the busy schedules, it would be a close call, because most guests planned to arrive just fifteen minutes before Stan probably would.

Jenna had hit a couple of last-minute snags, so she was running behind, too. After picking up Jordan, she zoomed to Stan's to find the guests waiting behind the building. Catching a few of the Bad Boys doing the secret handshake, she told them to leave the spitting outside. After a few smart remarks, she let everyone inside and with Jordan's help, set up food and drinks on Stan's dining room table.

"You want some help hanging that sign?" an unfamiliar voice offered.

Jenna glanced up from setting out the paper cups and stared at the tall man in front of her. His eyes and curly hair gave him away. She'd known him years ago when he'd lived down the street from her. "Max Derenger," she said. "You grew!"

He laughed. "Lord, I hope so. I was the skinniest, scrawniest kid on Cherry Lane, and I was always getting beat up."

"Well, you've obviously left that behind. I would love some help with the sign, since it's the *only* party decoration besides the balloons." She glanced at her watch and felt a jab of panic at the time. "Jordan, he should be here any minute. Would you mind being the lookout?"

"I was the lookout in the treehouse," Max informed her with a grin.

Jenna laughed. "I need your height for the sign."

While the rest of the guests talked among themselves, Max took one side of the sign and Jenna took the other. They hung it in the entrance to the den.

"This was a great idea to get a bunch of the guys from Cherry Lane for Stan's birthday. I haven't seen him in years. How did you find everyone?"

Jenna was pleased with her idea to reunite Stan with some of the bad boys. She knew how much he longed to feel more connected, so she'd hoped this would help. "It wasn't easy," she said. "I didn't have much time, and a lot of people have scattered. Kevin Saunders is in the Navy, and he's stationed in California right now. Joey Caruthers lives in Colorado. I'm not sure how he did it, but he made a lot of money, and now he runs some sort of charitable foundation for kids."

"Sounds like you've been busy," Max said, and gave her a thoughtful glance. "You and Stan must be pretty close."

Jenna's heart tightened and she hesitated. "I guess

you could say that,'' she said quietly, then changed the subject. ''What's been happening with you?''

Max grinned. ''I graduated from Tech with a degree in engineering, but along the way I got interested in karate. I teach at my own karate school.''

Jenna laughed and shook her head. ''Stan is going to love this. He—''

''He's coming!'' Jordan yelled. ''He just got out of his car!''

Jenna felt a rush of excitement. Several people made hushing noises. They all waited for the sound of Stan coming in the door.

Instead, there was the sound of footsteps in the hall leading to the bedroom. ''What's going on in here?'' a feminine voice called out.

A very attractive blond woman, dressed in a silky robe, rounded the corner from the bedroom and stared at the crowd with wide eyes. Since the guests were primarily men, they gaped at her with equal surprise.

''Hey, Jenna Jean, were you saving her for the cake?'' one wise guy cracked. ''Great addition to the party.''

''Party?'' the woman echoed sleepily. She'd obviously just woken up.

''*Who* is she?'' Max asked.

Jenna's mouth went dry. ''I don't know.''

Ben Palmer stepped forward and extended his hand. ''We're celebrating Stan's birthday. A little surprise party. I'm Ben. You're—''

''Brandi.'' Her face creased in confusion. ''Stan and I knew each other in Florida, and I thought I'd surprise him, too.''

It was clear from the way Brandi was dressed exactly *how* she planned to surprise Stan. Jenna couldn't swear what was beneath the woman's robe, but she suspected it wasn't much. She felt as if she'd been punched. No, it was worse than that.

The front door swung open, dragging everyone's attention from Brandi. Jenna distantly heard the chorus, "Surprise!"

Mass confusion followed. The room took on a surreal appearance. She felt as if she were having an out-of-body experience. Some part of her saw the surprise and delight on Stan's face as his boyhood friends crowded around him. Some part registered the sounds of laughter and male voices. Her feet, however, felt rooted to the floor.

She felt a tug on her arm and glanced at Jordan, who was looking at her with a worried expression on his face. "Are you okay?" he asked.

She forced her mouth to make a smile. "Of course."

"You don't look okay."

"I will," she said through gritted teeth.

"Do you want me to tell her to go away?"

The offer sliced past her defenses. The fierce protectiveness on Jordan's young face nearly brought tears to her eyes. She took a deep breath and squeezed his arm. "I think that might not be our job. I'm going to light the candles and make sure the drinks are ready."

"Are you mad at Stan?"

Jenna paused. She had to think about that. "Not mad," she said, but other emotions blasted through her relentlessly. Pain. Humiliation. Jenna had never been so hurt in her life. Brandi had said she wanted to surprise Stan, but Jenna couldn't help wondering about the relationship.

As she lit the candles on the cake, she tried not to think, but her mind shouted all her doubts. She should be fair and give Stan an opportunity to explain, her rational side insisted.

You were right. You couldn't hold him.

Jenna bit her lip and swallowed hard over the knot in her throat.

She glanced up to see Brandi giving Stan a birthday kiss, and something inside her broke. Her heart or her hope. Or both.

Looking surprised, he pulled back and glanced around the room until his gaze met hers. His eyes made the same promises he'd made last night, but Jenna couldn't get past the image of the scantily clad woman wrapped around him. He started to move toward her, and Jenna panicked. She couldn't deal with a public explanation right now. She needed to escape. She needed a diversion.

"Time for the cake," she said, and waved Jordan over. "Would you carry it to Stan while we sing?"

The group sang an enthusiastic though off-key rendition of "Happy Birthday," then Ben urged Stan to make a wish.

As soon as he blew out the candles, Stan lifted his gaze and headed for her again. Jenna's panic increased exponentially.

He put his arm around her, and Jenna couldn't help but stiffen.

Stan frowned. "We need to talk."

Jenna nodded. "I know, but this isn't a great time. We have an audience, and I need to cut the cake."

"This thing with Brandi," he told her. "It isn't the way it looks."

"Appearances can be deceiving," she agreed.

"You don't sound convinced."

"It's a little tough with her lipstick on your mouth."

He swore and rubbed his mouth with the back of his hand. "Jenna—"

She shook her head. "I'm not doing this in front of an audience," she whispered tersely. "You have guests, and I need to cut the cake." She deliberately moved away from him.

Jenna was able to force herself to remain at the party for seventeen more minutes before she just couldn't stand it any longer. Excusing herself to get more ice, she took a detour and silently escaped out the back door.

Breathing a sigh of relief, she leaned against the apartment building and stared at the darkening sky. Her mind was spinning faster than a top. She should pull herself together and return to the party, but Jenna was overspent. She knew she couldn't. She had to get away.

Spotting her white sedan, she made up her mind and walked swiftly toward it. Her purse was still in the apartment, but her keys jingled in her pocket. Her heart pounding, she stuck the key in the door and turned it.

"Jenna."

She jumped, turning quickly to face Jordan. "Hi," she managed to say.

"Why are you leaving?" he asked. "The party's not over."

"It is for me," Jenna said, pulling the door open. "I'm sure Stan won't mind if you stay with him or want a ride home."

"It's that lady, Brandi, isn't it?" His voice was full of scorn.

Jenna did not want to try to explain something that she hadn't sorted out for herself. "I just really need to go," she told him.

"Okay." He jammed his hands in his pockets. "You think I'll see you again?"

Jenna's wounded heart splintered again. She wouldn't have guessed because he wasn't one to express himself much emotionally, but he clearly hated the idea of losing another adult in his life.

"Oh, Jordan." Despite his resistance, she gave him a hug. "Of course you will." She felt her eyes burn with tears. "I just—" She swallowed and looked away. "Tonight's been a little much for me. Okay?"

He nodded. "Okay. Can I tell Stan?"

Jenna waffled; she didn't want to put Jordan in the middle. "I don't want his party spoiled."

"I'll tell him after it's over. Are you going home?"

At another time she might have been amused at the parental tone of his voice. "I'm not sure. But don't worry," she said, mustering a sad smile as she scooted into the car. "I'll go somewhere safe."

After Stan took Brandi aside and told her he was seriously involved with someone else, he gave Ben the assignment of consoling her.

"It's a terrible job," Ben said with a gleam in his eye, "but since it's your birthday…"

"Don't take advantage," Stan said.

"Not this time. But no promises if she comes to visit *me* instead of you."

Stan nodded, narrowing his eyes as he searched for Jenna. "Have you seen Jenna? I haven't spotted her in over five minutes."

"Beats me," Ben said with a shrug. "Maybe she's in the kitchen."

His intuition said different, but he decided to double-check anyway. "Maybe."

Although he was frequently stopped by one of the grown-up Bad Boys, Stan checked every room, including the closet and the pantry. With a bad feeling invading his gut, he returned to his den to find Jordan eating his third piece of cake and watching TV. "I'm looking for Jenna," Stan said.

"She's gone," Jordan said around a bite of cake.

"She's *gone*," Stan echoed, his sense of foreboding increasing. He'd known she was upset. Anyone could read it on her face. He'd wanted to take her aside and explain, most importantly, reassure her. He should have followed his instincts. Because she'd stayed, he'd thought it was under control. Now she'd slipped away. Stan began to sweat. He stepped in front of the TV screen. "Where? Where did she go?"

Jordan shrugged. "I dunno. She looked like she was gonna cry. She said she was going somewhere—" Jordan broke off and made a face. "Oops. She told me not to tell you she was gone until your party was over. She didn't want to ruin it."

His heart felt as if it had been ripped out. He could just imagine what Jenna was thinking. Stan turned away and plowed his fingers through his hair. He refused to lose her over something so stupid. He wouldn't lose her, he told himself, but Stan knew Jenna was a woman with a strong mind and tender heart. If she didn't believe him, he was dog meat.

Swearing under his breath, he returned to the room where his childhood friends were. Most had already left. To the few who remained, he waved to get their attention. "I really appreciate you guys coming to remind me how old I am and how stupid I used to be, but I've got a little emergency I need to take care of."

"Medical or personal?" Max prodded.

"Personal."

"Still trying to catch Jenna Jean after all these years," Max said with a commiserating grin.

"I'm not gonna just catch her," he told Max. "I'm gonna keep her."

Twelve

Sheer instinct led Jenna to Maddie's house. She pounded on the door, and when Maddie opened it, the two women just stared at each other.

Maddie found her voice first. "I thought the party was tonight."

Jenna nodded, feeling like she was held together by tissue paper. "It was."

"Why aren't you still there?"

The image of Brandi, blond and confident of Stan's interest, taunted her. "Change in plans. I realize I didn't call first, but do you mind if I hang around here for a while?"

"Of course I don't mind. Do you want to stay the night?"

"Or the week," Jenna murmured, following her friend into the house.

Maddie turned around to face her. "You have to tell me what's going on."

"If I do, I'll cry," Jenna said, feeling the dam holding back her tears crack.

Maddie frowned in concern, then paused thoughtfully. "Joshua, honey," she called. "Jenna and I are going for a walk."

Joshua peered around the corner. "It's dark. Where are you going?"

"My hill," she told him, and walked over to give him a kiss.

Jenna's heart twisted at the sight of their obvious love. She felt Joshua's probing gaze and offered a halfhearted smile. "Hi."

Clearly sensing something was wrong, he looked from one woman to the other. "Let me know if you need something."

Maddie smiled. "I will. We'll be back in a while." She grabbed a box of tissues and a blanket, then nudged Jenna out the door.

"*Your* hill?" Jenna prompted as she walked with her friend down a dirt road.

"It's a great place. Very peaceful," she told Jenna.

The sun had set, but the trees hid the stars until they walked to the top of a grassy hill. Despite her distress, the quiet beauty of the spot stunned her. "The stars look like diamonds," she said, awed.

"Or Austrian crystal," Maddie said, spreading out the blanket. "Spill it, Jenna. I haven't seen you this upset since you bit Stanley Michaels's hand and he had to get stitches."

Jenna closed her eyes, surprised at the force of her pain. "This time I feel like I need the stitches."

"You're not telling me why."

She took a deep breath. "Well, just before we were all going to yell 'Surprise!', this blonde comes out of his bedroom and..." With halting sentences and a breaking voice that echoed the state of her heart, Jenna filled Maddie in on the evening's events. Several times she had to stop, but each time, she paused and collected herself and continued.

Maddie, who usually chattered enough for ten people, remained quiet until the end. "Oh, Jenna," she gently said, shaking her head. "You have fallen completely in love with Stan."

"I know," she said, and felt her composure disintegrate. Tears streamed down her face. "I don't know what to do. I don't—" Her voice quit, and a sob broke from her throat.

Maddie offered her a tissue and put her arm around her shoulder. "Do you really think anything is going on between this Brandi woman and Stan?"

Jenna sniffed and wiped at tears that continued to fill her eyes. "I don't know," she wailed. "He looked surprised to see her. But, Maddie, she was very pretty. All the guys were staring at her with their mouths hanging open."

"That could have had something to do with how she was dressed," Maddie said dryly.

Jenna bit her lip and hiccuped. "Probably. But I would be a fool not to see that she and Stan have been involved. Sexually involved." She closed her eyes at the sick feeling in her stomach.

"And how does that make you feel?"

"Like throwing up."

Maddie squeezed her shoulder. "Jenna, you know he hasn't been a monk."

"I know. I know it, and part of my brain can accept it. But coming face-to-face with one of his past—" She stopped, the sick feeling taking over again.

Maddie sighed. "Do you want him?"

More confused than ever, she pulled another tissue from the box and wiped her eyes. "I don't know. I hate the way I feel right now."

Maddie's eyes filled with sympathy. "It's because you care so much. How do you feel when you're with him?"

Jenna's heart squeezed. "Happier than I've ever been in my life." She met Maddie's gaze. "This sucks."

Maddie smiled, then her face turned serious. "You need to decide if you can live with not being the very first woman in Stan's life."

Jenna made a frustrated sound. "I don't expect to be his first. That's not the—"

Maddie held up her hand. "I know. I'm wondering who you're really doubting now. Stan or yourself. But just think about this. It's not important that you're the first woman in Stan's life, as long as you're the last."

After two days of fruitlessly trying to see or talk to Jenna, Stan was half out of his mind. The night of the party he'd taken Jordan home, then he had parked in Jenna's driveway until the dark hours of the morning. When she hadn't come home, he was torn between worry for her safety and dread that she had turned her back on him. He'd driven past her house so many times he wondered when the neighbors would call in a complaint to the police.

He'd telephoned her at work a dozen times yesterday, but she hadn't taken his calls or returned them. Today was Saturday, and he was taking yet another drive past her house. Spotting her car in the driveway, he felt a rush of adrenaline. She was home.

He parked his car and was pounding on her door within two minutes flat.

"Just a minute," she called, and he was so impatient he counted while he waited.

Jenna opened the door, and Stan watched a flood of conflicting emotions cross her face.

His gut tightened. "I called you."

Clearly tense, she took a deep breath. "I know. I apologize. I— I—" She sighed. "I didn't know what to say."

"Let me in, and maybe I can help," he said.

She paused, and her reluctance cut at him. "Okay."

They walked together through the foyer where they'd first made love. The image vibrated through him. In those moments she had been his.

"I baked some cookies," she said halfheartedly. "Do you want any?"

For once in his life, Stan wasn't hungry. "Not now, thanks."

She nodded, then waved her hand for him to sit. She chose a chair.

Unwilling to dance around the issue any longer, Stan laid the facts on the table. "I haven't been involved with Brandi since I was in Florida. I never called her, once I moved here. She called me a few times, but I always told her I was busy. *No one* was more surprised that she showed up at my apartment than I was."

Jenna grimaced. "I don't know. Since I didn't know she even existed, I have to say I was pretty surprised." She hesitated a beat. "She's very pretty."

He narrowed his eyes. "I don't know what's going on in your head, but I haven't been involved with anyone but you since I moved to Roanoke."

She nodded slowly, but didn't look at him.

Stan's heart twisted. "You don't believe me."

Her head shot up. "I didn't say that. I'm just confused."

Impatient, Stan stood. He wanted things to be okay. He wanted her back. Immediately. "I don't see what's confusing. She showed up. I didn't invite her. I told her I'm involved with someone else. End of story."

Jenna bit her lip. "Maybe that's the way it should be, but—"

"But you don't believe me."

Her eyes flashed. "I didn't say that. It's just not that easy for me. It reminded me how different I am from the other women you've been involved with and—"

"That's good. The difference," he insisted between gritted teeth, "is good."

"Maybe it's good," she said with a forced shrug. "Maybe it's temporary and—"

Stan swore loudly.

Frustration creasing her face, she stood, too. "You make this sound like it should be so easy, but how would you have felt if some half-dressed man came strolling out of my bedroom when you were trying to give me a surprise party?''

The mere image infuriated him. At the same time it took a large slice out of his indignation. "I would have beat him to a pulp and sent him on his way."

She shot him a look of impatience. "I didn't think a catfight would be an appropriate addition to your party."

He struggled with his unhappiness and tried to push the conversation forward. "So what do we do? We have to get past this."

She nodded. "Yes, I do."

"You don't sound sure." The hurt confusion on her face tore him up. He stepped closer to her and put his hands on her shoulders. "Dammit, Jenna, I want you back. I want you to believe me."

Her eyes welled with tears, and she looked up at the ceiling. That scared the spit out of Stan. Jenna was *not* given to tears.

"I'm trying," she said in a tight, rusty voice. "I'm trying. I might not have a problem believing in you. I'm just not sure I can believe in me."

Stan looked into her eyes and felt his heart stop. The expression on her face leveled him more effectively than a bulldozer. She looked hopeless, and he had never felt more helpless.

They agreed to give Jenna two weeks, but with each passing day, Stan grew more downhearted. He couldn't remember when he'd been more miserable. Sitting in the grass beside the basketball court, he watched Jordan shoot hoops.

"Wanna play?" the kid asked.

Stan shook his head. "Not this time."

Jordan shrugged and dribbled the ball. "When are you gonna see Jenna again?"

Stan sighed. "I don't know. It's been four days. I don't know."

"Did you send her flowers or any of that stuff?"

"No. She says she's confused."

Jordan stopped bouncing the ball to stare quizzically at Stan. "Will flowers confuse her more?"

"No. I guess not." Stan rubbed his hand over his face. "I'm not sure they'll do any good." He changed the subject. "How are things going with your brother?"

"Okay. He's been home at night a little more lately."

"That's good."

"We talked about me coming to live with you."

Surprised, Stan studied Jordan. The kid was very careful with his emotions. He was shooting hoops again. "So, what'd you two have to say?"

"He said he might be an okay brother, but he wasn't too hot at this guardian stuff. He asked me if I wanted to live with you."

Stan kept his opinion to himself. "And?"

"I said I didn't want to lose my brother, but it was nice having an adult around when you need one."

Stan's lips twitched at Jordan's practical point of view.

"He said I wouldn't ever lose him as a brother. He said maybe we could work something out where I live with you, but I can still stay with him sometimes."

Jordan stopped and cradled the ball at his hip. He finally looked at Stan. "You haven't said much about me coming to live with you lately. Have you changed your mind?''

Stan's broken heart melted, and he walked over to Jordan. ''I didn't want to pressure you,'' he said, squeezing Jordan's shoulder. ''Are you too old for a hug?''

Jordan shrugged, but when Stan hugged the boy, he dropped the ball and hugged him back. ''I'm going to have to start doing some serious house hunting. Do you mind living in the apartment till then?''

Jordan shook his head. ''Nah, but I think we ought to get Jenna to let both of us stay in her house.''

Stan sighed. ''I don't know, Jordan. I'm not sure what she'll do.''

Jordan's face was earnest. ''Well, maybe you should remind her that she's yours. Sometimes people forget.''

On the fifth day since she had seen Stan, Jenna was still confused. She felt bad about her doubts, and she missed Stan. He'd become a vital part of her life. Did she really want to live without him?

The question plagued her night and day, but she resisted the urge to call him until she was sure. It wasn't fair to drag him down with her deep-seated uncertainty.

A package was delivered to her at work while she was in court. With mixed feelings of anticipation and reluctance, she closed her door and opened the box.

A white hat.

Her heart twisted. It said so much. Another man might have sent flowers, but Stan sent a white hat to remind her that he believed in her, even if she didn't believe in herself quite yet. Jenna burst into tears.

It took her so long to conceal her red eyes that the next day when a package arrived, she was afraid to open it. Taking a deep breath, she opened the flat envelope to find a photo of her and Stan at the Youth League Day at the lake. It was after he'd thrown her into the lake and dragged her out. Though she was drenched, she wore a reluctant smile. Laughing, Stan held her in his arms. She looked like she belonged there, in his arms. Jenna kept the picture in her top drawer.

The third day another box arrived, and she was curious. It was an elaborate tiara, appropriate for a queen. A little laugh squeezed past her tight throat as she recalled the smaller one Emily had shared with her and Maddie as children. She'd had so many dreams then, some she hadn't even admitted to herself.

Stan was one of those secret dreams. Not the Stan from years ago, but the man he'd become. The man who loved her enough to keep telling her.

Jenna felt something inside her shift. Everything seemed to click into place. It was such a monumental sensation she glanced outside to see if the sun had come out. Still cloudy, she noted, but not inside her.

Everything was suddenly crystal clear. Stan loved her. She loved him. He wanted to help make her dreams come true.

Maybe it was time, she thought, as she held the tiara in her hand, for her to make some of *his* dreams come true.

* * *

Stan was so nervous he was perspiring. "Are you sure it's okay if you stay with your brother tonight?"

"No problem," Jordan said. "I can ride my bike, and you won't—"

"I don't like you riding your bike on Hershberger Road. Too much traffic."

"I've done it for months."

"You should wear a helmet, too."

Jordan made a face. "They look hot."

"A skull cast is a lot hotter," Stan told him.

"Are you this cranky because you're going to see Jenna tonight?"

Stan took a deep breath. "Yes," he admitted. "But I'm still buying a bike helmet for you, and I want you to wear it."

"Are you and Jenna gonna have a lot of rules?" Jordan asked warily.

"Yes." Stan didn't pull any punches. "Do you think you'll be able to live with that?"

Jordan hesitated and shrugged. "I can put up with a lot for her cookies."

Stan laughed and rubbed Jordan's head. He drove Jordan to his brother's and returned to his apartment. Jenna had asked if she could meet him there. He wondered at the possible implications and decided he was driving himself crazy for nothing. He chugged down a beer and wished it were Scotch.

She rang the doorbell on time. His heart hammered in his chest. A prompt woman. She was a rarity in so many ways. He opened the door. She was dressed in a black and hot pink sundress, and her eyes were bright with anticipation. He couldn't tell if she was excited or nervous, but she was smiling. The double knot of tension in his stomach loosened slightly.

"Are you ready?" she asked.

"I guess. You want to come inside?"

She shook her head. "No. I thought we'd talk somewhere else."

Curious, but unwilling to rock the boat at this point, he shrugged. "Okay. I'll drive."

"No," she said again, and smiled. Her gaze made promises that turned his heart over. "I will."

She turned, and he narrowed his eyes, wondering for the thousandth time what was going on inside her sexy, female brain. He locked up and joined her outside. It was a dark, starless night. He found himself looking for at least one star so he could make a wish as they got into her car.

"Thank you for the white hat," she said, pulling out of the complex.

"I thought it suited you," he said, struggling with his need to touch her.

"The other women lawyers in the office are jealous."

"Of the tiara?"

Jenna shook her head and smiled a mysterious smile. "No. They're jealous of the man in the picture you sent me."

"Oh." Stan tread softly. "Is that good or bad?"

She lifted one shoulder and shook her head. "Neither. It doesn't really matter what they think." She pulled to a stop at a light. "Would you do me a favor?"

"Sure."

She reached behind her and put a scarf into his lap. "Would you cover your eyes with this?"

Holding the silk between his fingers, he stared at her in confusion. "What?"

"Cover your eyes. Hurry. Or it will be too late." The light changed and she turned left.

"What is this—"

"Stan, I know that since you're a doctor, you have just as much difficulty with control issues as I do, but would you please just put on the blindfold?"

Reluctant, he swore, but did as she asked.

"Can you see?"

"No," he said, his tone curt to his own ears. Stan had been living in a state of complete emotional frustration for the past week, and his patience was paper thin. He'd felt out of control for days. The blindfold just made matters worse.

"Good." She squeezed his leg reassuringly. "It's just for a few minutes."

"It better be," he muttered.

She turned on the radio and continued to drive. He felt the car take several winding curves before she pulled to a stop.

He reached for the blindfold, but her hand covered his.

"Not yet. Just a little longer."

Giving a long sigh, he heard her pull something from the back seat and slam her door. She opened his door and guided him. He noticed it was cooler and the wind whipped around them. He walked on pavement, then his feet encountered softer ground and leaves.

She brought him to a stop. "Before you take off the blindfold—"

"You mean I have to wait *longer?*"

"Would you shut up so I can tell you that I love you?"

Stunned into silence, Stan ripped the scarf off his head and stared at Jenna. She looked somewhere between peeved and nervous.

His heart pounded against his rib cage. "Would you repeat that?"

"Didn't you hear me the first time?"

"Yeah, I did," he said in a rough voice as he pulled her into his arms. "But I want to hear it again."

"I love you," she told him, and the certainty in her eyes filled up all his empty, hurting places. "Have you noticed where you are?"

He shook his head. "I'm too busy looking at you."

Her blue gaze grew shiny with unshed tears. "I can't believe how lucky I am that you love me."

"It works both ways, Jenna Jean."

She stroked his cheek. "There's something else I want to ask you. It's important, and if you need some time I'll understand." She took a short, quick breath. "Will you—"

Alarm rushed through him and he pressed his hand over her mouth. "Oh, no you don't!" He swore under his breath. This woman would keep him on his toes for the rest of his life. "I've been wanting to ask you for the past month, but I didn't think you were ready. You are not pulling this rug out from under me. You've been mine for a while, Jenna. You just didn't know it. Will you marry me?"

Her eyes widened and she dipped her head, her voice muffled by his fingers. "That better be yes," Stan said, and pulled his hand away.

"Yes, yes, yes," she said, and lifted her mouth to his. Stan could barely breathe, his heart was so full. He had never felt so complete in his entire life. He reacquainted himself with her taste. He ran his fingers through the silk of her hair and pulled her against him, as close as he could bring her.

When they came up for air, her expression was slightly dazed. "You still don't know where you are," she murmured.

Tearing his gaze from her, he looked around and saw the lights of Roanoke beneath them. He glanced to the side and saw the Mill Mountain Star. Remembering he'd told her his little fantasy, he looked back at Jenna. His body tightened at her expression. "I hope you brought a blanket."

"It's already on the ground," she told him, and pulled him back for another kiss.

Arousal kicked through him like wildfire. Despite the coolness of the night, she was warm and eager. "Oh, man, Jenna are you sure you want to do this?" he asked against her mouth as he dragged her dress up her thighs.

"Yes." Tugging his shirt loose, she acted as if she felt the same urgency. They'd been away from each other too long. One night was too long. A week had seemed an eternity.

He slid his hands up to her bottom and found her naked. He groaned. "You're not wearing anything underneath," he said, rubbing his fingers over soft skin and taut muscle.

Feeling her unfasten his slacks, he took her hand and wrapped her fingers around him intimately.

"I love you," she whispered as she stroked him. "I want to make all your dreams come true."

His heart was full, his body vibrating with need. The need to show her, to possess her. "You already have."

They tumbled to the blanket, and Jenna wouldn't stop kissing him. Everywhere her lips touched him— his throat, his chest, his belly—he was branded by her. She flowed down his body like a hot wind, and stunned him when she took him into her mouth.

Her tongue and lips caressed him intimately, and Stan felt himself slipping toward the edge. "No, sweetheart," he said, drawing her up to him.

Her eyes were wild with need, wanton and full of love.

Stan rolled her gently beneath him, and as he slid inside her soft warmth, he knew that she was his. And he was hers.

Later they lay wrapped in each others arms with the blanket pulled around them. Beyond Jenna, Stan could see the Mill Mountain Star. He shook his head and looked at her. "I love you. Do you know that?"

Jenna sighed and nodded. "You'd better, considering the fact that I just committed a felony under the Mill Mountain Star with you."

Epilogue

Four months later Jenna Jean Anderson and Stanley Michaels were married in a little chapel on Mill Mountain. The reception was held at the Hotel Roanoke, and all the important people attended.

Maddie and her husband, Joshua, spent most of their time preventing Davey from eating too many cookies. Jordan, who had been living with Stan for a while, and Joshua's son, Patrick, traded opinions on basketball teams. Jenna's family enveloped Stan's mother so that it was difficult to tell where one family ended and the other began.

Emily, now seven months pregnant, was alternately urged to be seated by her handsome, hovering husband, Beau, and her mother. She had yet to take a chair.

The only guests who were pushing their luck were

the grown-up members of *The Bad Boys Club*. Halfway through the reception, Jenna was dancing with Stan. "I love you more than life, but if you guys do that disgusting handshake at this reception, I'm leaving without you."

He laughed. "Don't worry," he told her, and kissed her.

The joy in the room overflowed. There was laughter and smiles on all the faces. It was still hard for Jenna to believe how wonderful life had become for her.

Maddie and Emily came to her side, both hugging her at the same time. "I'm so happy for you," Emily said. "How does it feel being a grown-up princess?"

Jenna smiled, so happy that tears were threatening. "Queen, remember?"

Maddie laughed. "I want to know what he tells people about the scar on his hand."

Glancing at her new husband, Jenna grinned. "He says he can't wait to tell everyone his *wife* did it."

Surrounded by some of the recently reacquainted Bad Boys, Ben lifted his glass in a toast. "To Stan. It took you about twenty years, but you finally caught Jenna Jean Anderson."

"And now I'm going to keep her," Stan replied.

"Here, here," the group said.

Then Jenna watched in disgust as they performed their secret handshake. She shook her head. "I warned him," she said.

Maddie looked at her in concern. "Warned him about what?"

Jenna grabbed her bouquet and headed for the double doors leading out of the room. Her friends trotted along beside her. "I warned him that if they did that gross handshake at the reception, I would leave without him."

Waddling as fast as she could, Emily gasped. "You're not really going to leave, are you?"

"He'll never believe me if I don't carry through," she said. Although the wedding and reception had been wonderful, she'd had enough. "I'll be fighting this my entire life. No, thank you."

"She's got a point," Maddie said.

"Jenna Jean, where are you going?" Stan called out.

Jenna kept walking. "To the bar," she called over her shoulder. "Feel free to spit all you want."

Hearing him swear, she picked up her pace.

"You're not leaving this reception without me," he told her, catching up with her.

"Yes, I am. You can't make me stay. You can't make—"

He hauled her over his shoulder, knocking the breath out of her. He turned back toward the room.

"This is ridiculous," Jenna said, but she couldn't smother her laughter when she saw the shock and amusement on the faces of the wedding guests.

"Sweetheart, when it comes to you, you'd be surprised how ridiculous I can get. Now throw that bouquet, so we can get out of here," he told her. "G'night everybody. Thanks for coming."

Titters and guffaws filled the room.

"There you go giving orders again," Jenna said.

"Jenna, there's a bathtub of champagne waiting in

our suite. I've got plans for you. Throw the damn bouquet.''

And Jenna threw the bouquet.

*   *   *   *   *

Bestselling author

JOAN
JOHNSTON

continues her wildly popular miniseries with an
all-new, longer-length novel

The Virgin Groom
HAWK'S
WAY

One minute, Mac Macready was a living legend in
Texas—every kid's idol, every man's envy, every
woman's fantasy. The next, his fiancée dumped him,
his career was hanging in the balance and his future
was looking mighty uncertain. Then there was the
matter of his scandalous secret, which didn't stand a
chance of staying a secret. So would he succumb to
Jewel Whitelaw's shocking proposal—or take cold
showers for the rest of the long, hot summer…?

Available August 1997
wherever Silhouette books are sold.

Silhouette®

Take 4 bestselling love stories FREE

Plus get a FREE surprise gift!

Silhouette makes it easy to heat up those long summer nights!

Clip the attached coupon and receive 50¢ off the purchase of *Hawk's Way: The Virgin Groom* by bestselling author Joan Johnston!

Available August 1997, wherever Silhouette books are sold.

Silhouette®
™

New York Times bestselling author

LINDA LAEL MILLER

Two separate worlds, denied by destiny.

THERE AND NOW

Elizabeth McCartney returns to her centuries-old family home
in search of refuge—never dreaming escape would lie over a
threshold. She is taken back one hundred years into the past and
into the bedroom of the very handsome Dr. Jonathan Fortner,
who demands an explanation from his T-shirt-clad "guest."

But Elizabeth has no *reasonable* explanation to offer.

Available in July 1997 at your favorite retail outlet.

MIRA The brightest star in women's fiction

SILHOUETTE® Desire®

COMING NEXT MONTH

#1087 NOBODY'S PRINCESS—Jennifer Greene

Alex Brennan, August's *Man of the Month,* was a white knight looking for a fair maiden to love. Regan Stuart was a beauty who needed someone to awaken her sleeping desires...and Alex was more than willing to rescue this damsel in distress.

#1088 TEXAS GLORY—Joan Elliott Pickart

Family Men

Posing as sexy Bram Bishop's wife was the closest to marriage headstrong Glory Carson ever wanted to come. But it didn't take much acting to pretend that the most wanted bachelor in Texas was the prince of her dreams.

#1089 ANYBODY'S DAD— Amy Fetzer

Mother-to-be Tessa Lightfoot's solo baby parenting plans didn't include Chase Madison, the unsuspecting sperm bank daddy. But if Tessa didn't keep him out of her life, she didn't know how much longer she could keep him out of her bed.

#1090 A LITTLE TEXAS TWO-STEP—Peggy Moreland

Trouble in Texas

Leighanna Farrow wanted a home, a family and a man who believed in happily-ever-after. Hank Braden wanted Leighanna. Now, the sexiest, most confirmed bachelor in Temptation, Texas, was about to learn what this marriage business was all about....

#1091 THE HONEYMOON HOUSE—Patty Salier

For better or worse, Danielle Ford had to share close quarters with her brazenly male colleague, Paul Richards. And his sizzling overtures were driving her to dream of her own honeymoon house.

#1092 UNEXPECTED FATHER—Kelly Jamison

Jordan McClennon was used to getting what he wanted, and he wanted former flame Hannah Brewster and the little boy he thought was their son. But when the truth came out, would it change how he felt about this ready-made family?